Christopher Higgins is a resident of Montgomery County, Pennsylvania. His interest in the Civil War stems from a young age, having visited Gettysburg as a boy (and countless times thereafter). Other sites he has travelled to include Antietam National Battlefield, Boone Hall Plantation, Ford's Theatre, Harpers Ferry, and Fort Sumter. He is the proud descendant of Balthasar Moeckel, a German immigrant who served in Pennsylvania's 75th Regiment at the beginning of the war.

In his free time, Christopher enjoys spending time with his friends and family, reading, watching movies and cheering on the Philadelphia sports teams. As a young student, writing was a valuable outlet for him to escape and delve into his imagination. Since then, his passion has only grown stronger. He credits his family, friends, teachers, and professors for helping him to evolve as a writer, and he wishes to continue to improve his skills in years to come.

FADING SUN

Christopher Higgins

FADING SUN

Vanguard Press

VANGUARD PAPERBACK

© Copyright 2024
Christopher Higgins

A CIP catalogue record for this title is
available from the British Library.

ISBN 978 1 80016 644 8

Vanguard Press is an imprint of
Pegasus Elliot Mackenzie Publishers Ltd.
www.pegasuspublishers.com

First Published in 2024

Vanguard Press
Sheraton House Castle Park
Cambridge England

Printed & Bound in Great Britain

Dedication

For Mom and Dad.

PART I

Chapter 1

Shady Grove, Virginia
June 11, 1860

The world spun too fast for Thomas McLeary. He sat on a rocking chair at his front porch, a cigar wedged in between his lips, and puffed furiously. As he gazed upon a purple sky and a setting sun, he could do nothing more than shake his head in disgust.

How could a world that was so rich in natural beauty be home to men who were so selfish and stubborn?

No, he corrected himself. *That ain't the matter*.

As far as McLeary was concerned, there were two worlds. There was a world of his own, in which he could hold a cigar in one hand and a beer in the other, and then there was the 'other'. A world full of loud-mouths and nay-sayers, which he was forced to enter once a week when he left the comforts of home and rode to the local market. More and more, it seemed as if the former was becoming lost to the latter, and such an encroachment left a bitter taste in his mouth.

He took the cigar out of his mouth and exhaled deeply. *I done my time*, he thought. *I should not care no more.*

At sixty-four years of age, McLeary only wanted to be left in peace. Rough lines were etched along his brow, which had become furrowed and strained by years of hard labor. Dark brown eyes, stern and narrow, locked themselves upon lush grasses and gently sloped hills. Grey scruff ran down his cheeks and along his chin, forming a patchy beard that he had not bothered to groom. Strands of white hair poked out from beneath his straw hat and swayed slightly in the gentle breeze. Although he had not been in business for several years, McLeary refused to allow old habits to die. He wore the same outfit that he had always worn during his days as a tobacco farmer: tattered, grass-stained overalls, a wrinkled white cotton shirt rolled up to the elbows, and mud-stained brown leather boots.

The front door creaked open.

"Oh, there you are, Thomas," Alice McLeary chirped. "I was looking all over for you. Thought you ran off."

McLeary grunted, his eyes still trained upon the tranquil landscape. When her husband refused to crack a smile, Alice's cheerful demeanor fell slightly.

"Now then," she began as she strolled over and seated herself in the chair beside him. "What ails Thomas McLeary so much so that he doesn't even bother to offer a smirk?"

He took another puff of his cigar and let the smoke drift out in front of him like a fog.

"Thomas," she said softly. "What's wrong?"

McLeary cast a glance at his wife. Her silver hair was wrapped neatly in a bun, and she wore a light blue summer dress. She was a product of high society, a true southern belle: well-mannered, highly educated, and a Virginia girl through-and-through. As a young man, he had nearly fallen over backwards the day he found out that she had taken a liking to him. What was even more startling was when her father, a respectable lawyer who had enjoyed a place among Richmond's elite, had approved of their marriage. Not that McLeary had any grounds to complain, of course, but he could only wonder if the reason why he had approved was due to the fact that he was never found without a pipe in his hand.

There were countless tobacco farmers in the state, but by the grace of God, he had held McLeary's products in the highest regard. That was what mattered more than anything, McLeary had concluded long ago, and he had lived a life with a woman who was unlike any other. Even now, as she stared at him with soft, gentle hazel eyes, his frustration began to fade.

"It don' matter much, hon," McLeary said.

"You can tell me," Alice urged. "You haven't been the same since you returned from the market. What happened?"

"Don' worry 'bout it."

"Thomas."

Another puff. He rolled the cigar between his fingers before tossing it to the ground and crushing it with his foot.

"The world's jest changin', Alice," he stated, "that be all."

"The world's always changing," she nodded, adding with a smirk, "and you're getting older."

"I suppose," he remarked. "We *both* be gettin' older."

Alice laughed. "That's the truth of it!"

For a while, only the whisper of the breeze came to their ears.

"More treble 'n town today," McLeary began, his voice low and serious. "A young feller, northerner he was, came by 'n' started yoopin' 'n' yellin' all 'bout the need for big government."

"Oh my." Alice shook her head. "I reckon that didn't end very well for him."

"No," was the response. "Next thing ye know, Powell comes runnin' over 'n' gives him a piece o' his mind. And ye know Powell — he got that big mouth o' his 'n' that plantation — he starts tellin' him to take his thoughts 'n' crawl back up to Conneticit or Mass'chusetts or wherever he be from. I darn near thought them two was 'bout to send fists flyin'."

Alice's eyes widened. "There was a fight?"

"Almost," he replied. "The young man had nuff wits 'bout him to get goin'. He was lookin' for one, that be certain. Fact o' the matter was Powell was just 'bout ready to give it to him."

"Thank heavens things didn't get too out of hand."

"I agree," McLeary nodded, "but I'll tell ya somethin', Alice: that ain't the first time this sorta thang's been happenin'."

"I'd imagine so," she said sadly. "Ever since that mess at Harpers Ferry, this country hasn't been the same."

"No, it ain't."

Crickets chirped in the cool night air.

"Maybe we should get out of here while we're still in good health," Alice joked. "I hear England's weather is pleasant this time of year."

"My father was right," McLeary muttered. "Nothin' good ever woulda come from a government where men ruled 'emselves."

"He never was a believer in 'We the People', was he?"

"Nope." He shook his head. "If my father had it his way, this country'd still be flyin' under a British flag." McLeary shrugged. "O' course," he continued, "if I had it *my* way, everybody'd have nuff sense 'bout them to mind their own business."

"You'll see no argument from me."

"The nerve o' some people," McLeary fumed, "thinkin' they can come down here 'n' start tellin' us how we should be livin'."

"Don't take it personal, Thomas," his wife advised him. "Whoever ventured all the way down here was set on bringing nothing but trouble."

"That be the truth, Alice," he acknowledged, "but more 'n' more we been seein' folks thinkin' they is bigger 'n the law. You was sayin' 'bout that 'venture' John Brown put together. Well, I reckon, nay, *fear* there be more John Browns to come…"

"Oh, I would certainly hope not!"

"So'd I," he said, "but given where we's standin', I see the truth plainly - 'n' an ugly truth it be."

"Well," Alice declared, "if someone was to try something like that again, here's hoping a stop would be put to it before it even began."

"Yes, ma'am," McLeary agreed. "Lemme tell ye somethin' else: any John Brown who finds hisself on my porch'll be greeted by the barrel o' my gun… 'n' I'll shoot the bastard dead!"

Alice swatted his wrist. "Thomas McLeary!" she snapped at him. "Don't say such things!"

"Ain't mean nothin' by it."

"Mean it or not," she said, standing up, "you shouldn't be thinking such wicked thoughts. You have a right to be angry — that much I'll grant you, but making that kind of a threat is unacceptable. Not to mention your language… You're a better man than that."

"Sorry, darlin'." he reached for her hand. "It ain't my intention makin' ye upset."

Alice pulled away and started for the door.

"Just come to bed when you've settled down."

More crickets.

McLeary reached into his pocket and pulled out matches and another cigar. It was going to be a long night.

Chapter 2

Philadelphia, Pennsylvania
June 13, 1860

The world spun too slow for Erich Streicher. As droves of pedestrians scurried past his window, wrapped up in their own little worlds, he remained fixed at his desk with pen in hand. He stared down at a blank piece of paper. When the day was young, a blank page provided a sort of fresh optimism, a chance to allow his creative thoughts to flow freely and have their fun. But in the waning hours of the afternoon, when the shop was merely minutes away from closing its doors, his pitiful lack of progress left a knot in his stomach. The paper taunted him, or so it seemed.

Yet another day in the books as a 'promising' young writer for the *Freedom Fightin' Firebrands*.

Streicher sighed as he reclined in his chair and cast his gaze out the window. Flashy streaks of a bright sun slipped past narrow chimneys and towering brick factories and kissed the glass beside him. Day in and day out, it was always the same: the world seemed to pass him by.

It was no secret why he was tucked away in the cramped, mold-infested room that had once served as an old coat closet. He was the youngest, most inexperienced writer in the business, and as such his superiors found it appropriate that he would have to 'prove his worth' by working in solitude.

Numbingly frigid in winter and downright suffocating in summer, the dingy one-person work area had terribly deplorable conditions, so much so that he had grown ill on several occasions. At twenty-three years of age, he had the curse (so he thought) of being born with a resilient constitution, which gradually restored his health and brought him back to the office. Back to the place where he was shackled by monotony.

The day's assignment was simple, his boss had claimed. Shane Doyle, the pot-bellied, red-nosed Irishman had a knack for setting off a political fire.

"We need to get the pot stirring again, lad," Doyle had said. "I want a full-page work that rallies around abolition. Make it bold, unapologetic. I want every head that's south of the Mason-Dixon to be turned upside down once they hear what we've got."

For a moment, Streicher had stared in silent amusement at the short, plump gentleman with swollen cheeks and pudgy fingers. His face was fiery red, which seemed appropriate considering his fierce passion for political debate. A balding hairline suggested that his years were catching up to him, but Streicher preferred to think that his brown curls had been ripped out from all the times that he ran his fingers through his scalp. While his size and appearance were almost comical, Doyle often let his tongue run wild. Many times his thunderous voice shook the walls. It was never a secret as to how he was feeling on any given day.

It was that same voice, booming and assertive, that startled the young German and caused him to spin around in his chair.

"Herr Streicher!" Doyle popped his head into the room and grinned. "How's my manifesto coming along?"

Streicher did his best to return the smile. "Progress is a demon at times," he said calmly, "but rest assured, sir, I'll have something that'll really get their blood boiling."

"I want it done by Saturday," the Irishman ordered. "That way I can take it to church with me the next day and have it blessed by the Almighty!"

"Wouldn't have it any other way, sir," Streicher remarked, careful to keep on his good side.

"Maybe if we're *really* blessed," Doyle rambled on, "the Lord will break open the earth and let Hell devour all of those soulless souls… except for the Negroes, of course."

"Of course."

"They've had quite a miserable lot in life, haven't they?"

"Yes, sir."

"Bound in chains," Doyle shook his head. "Forced to work all day, every day from sunrise to sunset. If it's so easy, then why don't those southern 'gentlemen' do the work themselves?"

"It's the nature of the system, I'm afraid."

"It's an evil system, at that," he spat bitterly. His boisterous, whimsical demeanor was replaced by grim frustration as his cheeks sank to a dark red. Speaking with Doyle was like handling a fuse: when lit, there was no stopping it — one could only try to contain it. And Streicher knew that the only way to simmer down his hot-headed boss was to concur with his eccentric rants.

"Sir, I do believe that…"

"Southern *gentlemen*," he said, seething, "is what they call themselves. Do you know what they are?"

Streicher rattled off the answer in his head, careful not to roll his eyes. 'Savages, brutes, the likes of which have never before been seen on this earth…'

"Hypocrites, is what they are," Doyle ranted. "They go to church every week convinced that they're the Lord's angels, and yet they condemn their fellow men to a life of servitude and hardship. And they cry out… Oh, do they cry out… 'But what about *our* rights', they say. 'Slavery is a *legal* institution', they insist. Well, it is a great tragedy that this country continues to allow such evils to persist! But to the planter, the money-hungry devil that he is, I ask, who do you owe a greater allegiance to — the Lord or the United States?

There is no defense for slavery. *None*. The wallets of those pigs have been lined by the blood and sweat of Negroes. Their stomachs, too, have been filled by the Negroes, who cook and care for them. I don't give a rat's ass what anyone says — slavery has persisted for one reason only: *greed*. But I'll tell you this, lad, in this country the Negro and the White Man may not be equal... but they both end up in the same grave, when all is said and done. And damned be any man who rounds up his fellow men and treats them as if they were cattle. The Lord will see to that, I can promise you for certain!"

Silence festered in the stale air.

Yet another rousing speech gave by the sharp-tongued Irishman. Streicher nodded his head slowly and pretended to be wrapped up in thought. The truth of the matter was that despite his boss's passionate rhetoric, he never carried much of an opinion on slavery. Being the son of immigrants, he had not seen much of the New World, and he did not care to travel beyond the comforts of his native Germantown. For Streicher, the American South was simply a name, a vague region of the country that he had yet to lay eyes on. The very thought of a Negro in chains was strange and foreign, which often led his imagination astray. While he often churned out articles that were practically blasphemous to southern planters, he was unwilling to take his own bait.

Shane Doyle, more than anyone else he had ever known, was a radical. A radical with an agenda. A radical with a pen... and several employees who were willing enough to get his delusional thoughts printed in bold. And although he would never share his belief with Doyle, the young man knew an important truth. An irreconcilable truth.

The White Man was superior to the Negro.

There was no shame in admitting such a statement, so long as it was done when he was out of the office. Save for the Shane Doyles of the world, any rational person would have agreed that the Negro was different. He looked different than the White Man; he spoke differently too. On Sundays, the bells in their churches would ring out and awaken the whole city. A lively, rambunctious chorus of singing and laughter often tested Streicher's patience. "Mein Gott," he often muttered as he walked past. "Ruhe, bitte!"

"Streicher!" Doyle's voice stirred him awake. His boss stared at him expectantly. "Did you get a word of what I said?"

"No, sir," the young man confessed. "My apologies... I must have..."

"Got tired of my rambling, eh?" Doyle grinned.

That was the truth of it. "Sir, I..."

"Don't fret, lad," the Irishman waved his hand. "My wife has a habit of turning her head the moment I open my mouth. I spout off far more than I probably should. For all the hollering I do, it's a wonder she still bothers to keep me around."

It was Streicher's turn to grin.

"Anyway," Doyle continued, "what I was saying was that if you're having trouble putting that pen of yours to work, then maybe you need a little push. Take a trip over to the library tomorrow and have yourself a look around. I take it you're familiar with the abolitionists' latest weapon, *Uncle Tom's Cabin*?"

"Only by name, sir," Streicher answered honestly. "I've never read it myself."

"Give it a read, will you?" Doyle requested. His grin stretched wider. "That'll be sure to get your mind going."

"It's a good work, sir?"

"Damn good work!" his eyes lit up. "A master classic is what it is. It exposes those power-hungry, slave-whipping devils for what they are... a bunch of power-hungry, slave-whipping devils!"

"I look forward to reading it myself then," Streicher answered with forced enthusiasm.

"Good!" the Irishman's voice rang out. "And I look forward to seeing what kind of a storm you cook up."

"I won't disappoint you, sir."

"I know that," was the response. "You're awfully good with that pen of yours."

"Thank you, sir."

"Now if you'll excuse me," Doyle said as he reached into his pocket and glanced at his watch, "I must be off. The Mrs is expecting me for dinner tonight."

"Of course."

"Have a good night, lad."

"You as well, sir."

Doyle nodded politely, offered one last mischievous smile, and strode down the hallway. When the patter of his steps grew softer and the front door closed, Streicher hoisted himself to his feet. His parents would be expecting him for dinner, and there were chores to be done in the old house. A leaking roof needed to be patched up and flimsy floorboards needed to be replaced...

Streicher sighed as he strode out the front door and into the bustling street. It was going to be a long night.

Chapter 3

McLeary never considered himself to be the perfect gentleman. A tailored suit and polished shoes were foreign to a man who walked out of the house each day with tattered overalls and mud-caked boots. Such was the life of a tobacco farmer.

Tonight's occasion was unusual, to say the least. A black jacket rested upon his slim frame, and with every stride he took, the tails brushed against the backs of his legs, much to his displeasure. His pants, pressed and fitted to his figure, scratched at his skin. Black shoes, which reflected brightly against the orange sunlight, crammed his toes and rubbed against his heels. How any man could sport such attire regularly, McLeary would never know. Virginia's high society was truly one of a kind, and while he admired Alice's grace and elegance, it was her refined taste that tugged at his nerves tonight.

She had refused to let him leave the house without his top hat. After much back and forth, and McLeary's insistence that he would look like 'a slap-happy puppet' with it on, his wife took it upon herself to put the hat on for him. Then came the 'hairy' situation, in which Alice had requested that he shave his beard.

"Fer cryin' out loud," McLeary had protested, "we only gonna be out one night! I gotta live with myself after this, Alice, ye understan'?"

A compromise had been reached instead. McLeary agreed to trim the beard with the promise that he would be allowed to grow it out again. It was somewhat perplexing, he could not deny, how Alice's calm, reserved demeanor often became stern (and even demanding) whenever they embarked for a night on the town. Yet another reason why the farmer often insisted that they were better off enjoying the comfort of their own home.

Rather than spending the evening at his porch, puffing away on one of his hand-rolled cigars, he sat with arms folded in a horse-drawn carriage as it jostled and swayed down a worn-out dirt path. Alice sat beside him and looked out the window at the towering trees that slipped past them as they rode on. She wore her hair in a bun, and a purple dress fit elegantly upon her petite figure. A pair of silver earrings, each with a sparkling stone in the center, shone brightly against the setting sun. In her lap rested a small tin box, which contained cigars that McLeary had made himself. It was a gesture of gratitude that was made more on Alice's behalf than his; he did not believe that thanks needed to be given at all. More than anything, he was suspicious of their host's motives.

Henry Powell, one of the few planters in Shady Grove, had invited the couple for an evening of dinner and drinks. The gesture was an unexpected one, considering that McLeary thought of the gentleman as being nothing more than a friendly face. Each week at the market, the two men would exchange pleasantries, but their conversations were brief. Powell, with his loud mouth and everlasting social graces, preferred to have the attention of those who cheered him on.

Every person in Shady Grove knew Powell. It was his unmatched charisma that drew many laughs, and his witty knack for negotiation time and time again resulted in handshakes. The veteran planter, with his years of know-how and professional savvy, had served as a decorated colonel and war hero during the Mexican War. Rumors circled that he even thwarted several Indian raids during the campaign, which only added to his stellar resume.

If he wanted to run for political office, Powell would have won in a landslide. Be it on a local, state, or national level, he fit the bill for what people wanted. There were undoubtedly hundreds who wished that he would spare them even a few minutes' worth of conversation, but a man of his stature reserved the right to pick and choose who he shared an audience with. Which is why McLeary, the old hermit that he was, spent the ride pondering the reason for their visit.

What did Powell want with him? If it was to ask for a case of cigars, he went to an awful lot of trouble to do so…

A violent shake stirred him from his thoughts. The carriage had slowed considerably, and as the driver eased his grip on the reins, they came upon an iron gate. Past the gate, the road was flat and paved and led to a straightaway, where towering trees lined both sides.

The driver, a short and portly Negro dressed in a faded suit and top hat, turned an ear slightly in their direction and began to speak.

"We's almos' here, folks," he said cheerfully. "Just a leetle down de road a ways, we gonna come up te da house. Big ol' house. Pretty thang, it be."

McLeary glanced out the window. Further down the road, tucked away behind the trees, stood a large white mansion. Its tall, polished windows glistened, and marble pillars stood uniformly along the wide porch. There appeared to be, from what he could see, a large staircase that narrowed gradually as it ascended towards the entrance to the mansion. Two servants, their silhouettes etched along the front door, awaited them at the top step.

Powell's mansion was a town landmark of sorts. It was a palace. A world he called his own. Apparently, all of the smooth-talking and wallet-lining had quite literally paid off.

The driver spoke again. "Y'all never been te dis place, ain't dat right?"

"No, this is our first time," Alice responded.

"'N' likely our last…" McLeary muttered under his breath. Powell was up to something. He was sure of it.

He would not have bothered to entertain them if it was not worth *his* while. To engage in polite banter at a bustling market was one thing, but to be welcomed as royalty was something else entirely. Of all times, why *now* were they invited to spend an evening with him? Both Powell and McLeary had lived in Shady Grove their whole lives. If they were true friends, they would have spent many nights talking around a bottle of brandy or a case of cigars. But that had never been the case… until tonight.

"Well I think y'all gonna hava good time." The driver laughed. "Mas'r has dis place jumpin' almos' e'ry night in de summa. All sorts o' people comin' 'n' goin' all de time, ye know. Ain't never a quiet place."

The carriage pulled up to the entrance. Alice handed the cigar case to her husband and they strolled arm-in-arm up the staircase. The two servants greeted them with friendly smiles. A young Negro boy, about fifteen years old, sported a suit and delicately balanced a tray with two wine glasses. The other, a short, plump Negro woman with greying hair and round cheeks, wore a black dress and an apron.

"Good evenin', Missuh 'n' Mizzes MucLeary," the woman began. "Welcome to Missuh Powell's home. He be awfully happy to have ye tonight. Please, hava drink."

The boy extended the tray towards them. Alice took a glass and her husband held up his hand. "Nothin' fer me…"

"We're delighted to spend the evening with Mr. Powell, aren't we, Thomas?" Alice interrupted him.

She smiled up at him, but it was a forced gesture. Her eyes narrowed, which was enough for him to take the hint.

"Thanks," he mumbled as he reached for the other glass.

They were escorted inside to an entryway that was spacious and comfortable. Freshly painted white walls towered above them from all sides. A dark wooden floor, recently swept, stretched along the entirety of the room. At the far end, two winding staircases led up to the balcony of the second floor, where an iron rail overlooked all who came through the front doors. Past the balcony, a long corridor stretched into the recesses of the great house. Although he could not quite make out what lay beyond, McLeary assumed that it was the planter's private quarters.

On the first floor, two doors were propped open underneath the balcony, which revealed a bustling scene. Servants of all ages hurried about one way and another, carrying pots, plates, trays, and ingredients. One woman, McLeary saw plainly, squatted down and looked into the eyes of a little girl, who tried hard to avoid her gaze.

"Listen, child," the woman spoke, her voice gentle but firm, "I can't be havin' you runnin' all 'round here, ye understan'? You be gettin' hurt if you ain't careful."

"Sorry, mama," the girl responded meekly.

"Why don' you go to de back porch," the mother suggested, "'n' make sure everythin's tidy? We want everythin' nice 'n' good for Misstuh Powell."

The girl nodded her head and took off somewhere into the sea of chaos.

The old woman spoke up. "Please fergive us, folks; we's still tryin' to git dinna togetha. It takes many hands, ye understan'."

"Oh, it's quite alright," Alice said with a wave of her hand. "We have no doubt that it will be worth the wait."

McLeary sighed. He would have settled for only a drink if it meant that the night would end sooner.

"Ah, there they are!" a gruff voice rang out above them. "Mr. and Mrs. McLeary, what a pleasure it is to have you here tonight!"

Dressed from head to toe in a finely pressed grey suit, Henry Powell stood at the center of the balcony with his arms spread. With long legs, broad shoulders, and wide hips, he was a presence that could not be avoided. His full cheeks and round stomach were evidence that he never skipped any meals. A thick silver beard, tangled with curls, ran down to his chest. His hair matched the texture of his beard, and a grey hat rested atop his head.

His appearance was not complete without the proper accessories: golden cufflinks, a pocket watch, a white handkerchief, polished black shoes. When he strolled down the stairs and came towards them, a waft of cologne flooded McLeary's nostrils.

Powell gazed upon them and smiled, his teeth white and clean. The two men shook hands.

"My goodness, McLeary," Powell remarked, eyeing them up and down, "I invited you and the Mrs. over for dinner, and here you are dressed looking like you're about to meet the king of England. No need to outdo me in my own home, alright?"

Alice chuckled. McLeary tried to muster a laugh, but a half-smile came to his lips instead.

"We's pleased to be here, is all," McLeary said, trying to remember his manners. "Thanks fer havin' us, Henry."

"My pleasure!" the planter beamed. "And might I say…" Powell's eyes drifted towards Alice. He nodded politely. "Mrs McLeary," he continued, "it's been a while, hasn't it? You haven't aged a day, my dear. Beautiful as ever."

Alice blushed. "Why, thank you, Henry," she said. "It's a pleasure to see you again." She offered her hand and Powell gave it a kiss.

"We best be careful, shouldn't we?" He smirked. "If we keep this up, your husband will start to think that I'm taking you away from him."

The two of them laughed. McLeary rolled his eyes.

"Of course," Powell added, "my wife may have something to say about that as well. Speaking of which…" He glanced towards the empty balcony and then reached for his watch. "I apologize," the planter said. "I told her that she must be ready by the time the two of you get here. Well, you know how women can be; when they try on one dress, they have to try on four more. Isn't that right, Mrs. McLeary?"

He smiled and she returned the gesture. "I suppose that's the way it is sometimes," she said.

"Well then," Powell clasped his hands together, "I'm glad to see that the two of you have been served." He glanced over at the old woman beside them. "Rose," he said, "would you be so kind as to check on the Mrs. for me?"

She nodded. "Certainly."

As Rose made her way up the staircase, the planter turned his attention to the young boy.

"Now as for you, Sampson," Powell continued, "how about you escort Mrs. McLeary to the parlor? Get her whatever she wants, understand? It won't be much longer, Mrs. McLeary, until my wife joins you."

"Oh, that would be fine." Alice nodded. "And please, Henry, there's no need to stick to such formalities. Call me Alice."

"If you wish, Alice." Powell winked.

"We ain't joinin' our wives, Henry?" McLeary asked.

"We will for dinner," was the response, "but seeing as you brought that little treasure of yours…" He pointed to the tin box. "I figure you and I could have a cigar or two beforehand." He paused. "They are cigars, aren't they?"

"Yessir," McLeary answered. "Made 'em just fer you."

The farmer extended the box towards his host, who accepted it with enthusiasm. "You're a true gentleman, McLeary." Powell smiled. "I thank you, sir. Well, we wouldn't want such a treat to go to waste, would we? Let's have at them!"

***

The back porch overlooked a lush garden that held plants and flowers of all colors and sizes. Shades of red, orange, yellow, green, blue, and purple blended together to create a visual spectacle that was as much a work of art as it was a work of nature. It was a decorated display that was maintained by only the most tender of care. A small cobblestone path wound one way and then another, offering scenic views of the landscape ; no doubt it was a feature of the property that captured the eyes of many guests.

Beyond the garden was a sprawling green field, rich and freshly cut, that seemed to roll towards the orange horizon. The grasses swayed gently in the breeze and bathed in the warmth of a calm summer night. Dotted along the field were several small brick cabins that sat under the sun, and they glowed as its orange shadow swept past them. Each of the cabins had cracks and holes that exposed slivers of the interior. The bricks, which had once been freshly painted, were coated with dirt and dust and bore a hazy grey tint. It was apparent that the deterioration of the quarters was gradual, largely subjected to years of wear and tear by natural elements. Age was another factor, as the cabins had endured nearly three generations' worth of plantation life. A refurbishment was direly needed.

A cluster of Negroes, mainly young men and women, stood in the middle of the field and routinely went about their work, not paying any mind to the two men who observed them from afar. Unlike those who worked in the mansion, they wore faded, torn rags, and none of them had shoes. Several of the men were shirtless; their backs glistened in sweat as they raised their hoes and drove them into the earth with rapidity. The women carried pouches that ran down to their waists, which they used to hold cotton fibers as they milled about the white sea. They went about their work quickly and with purpose. As they busied themselves with their tasks, their voices sang out in unison:

> Hold ye breath
> Git down low
> Keep movin' keep movin'
> Jest don' go too slow

Look high in de sky
There a star be found
Reach fer it reach fer it
You no longer be bound

McLeary pulled the cigar out from his lips and let the smoke flood the air around him. Ever since he was a boy, he had known Negroes to be slaves. Yet it was a sight that even at his age made his eyes grow wide. There was something about the trade that made his stomach uneasy, but he could never point to the exact cause of it.

As far as he was concerned, he would never own a slave. Alice had fought against him about it once, but he would not budge. She had wanted a servant, particularly as they grew older, who could cook and tidy the house. But such an acquisition, he had argued, was not necessary for two people. They were better off spending their money on something else.

In exchange for her silence on the matter, McLeary had offered to take her on a trip to Richmond. The proposal had been met with enthusiasm, but every now and then she would hint that such a purchase was necessary and worthwhile.

"My goodness," Powell's thunderous voice echoed into the sky, "this cigar is su-perb! McLeary, you are a master of your craft!" The planter was seated in a chair several feet from him, puffing away happily and overlooking his property. After a moment, he rolled the cigar between his fingers and flashed the farmer a smile. "Let me tell you something, McLeary," he went on, "I've been all over the South and tried hundreds, if not thousands, of cigars. *Yours*, my good sir, are at the top. Dare I say they are the best in the whole country!"

"Thanks, Henry," the farmer muttered. Such compliments could not dismiss the fact that he so desperately wanted to be back on his own porch.

"Not that it matters much now," Powell began, "but back when you were in the business, did you ever consider buying more land?"

"No, sir," he answered honestly. "I ain't never wanted a big farm."

"I respect that," the planter said, nodding. "Less to manage, that's for certain."

"Yessir."

"I give you credit, McLeary," Powell remarked. "You've always been independent. Ran your business how you saw fit. Did all the planting yourself… If it's not too much to ask, why did you never get yourself a hand or two? I mean, purely for the sake of efficiency…"

"Niggers ain't cheap."

"Yes," Powell agreed as he fixed his eyes upon the choir in the field. "They do come with a heavy price."

"How many of 'em you got, Henry?"

"The Negroes?"

McLeary nodded.

"Twenty-five."

"That be a lot, ain't it?"

The planter chuckled.

"Well," he started, "in a town like Shady Grove, yes, I would say that's quite a lot. But if you go down a ways, say to South Carolina or Georgia, some of those boys own around a hundred."

McLeary's eyes widened. "*One hundred* of 'em, you say?" he asked. "That be damn near all o' Africa, ain't it?"

Powell nearly choked on his cigar. "Settle down, McLeary." He howled with laughter. "I never knew you were such a comedian. By the end of tonight, you'll give me a hernia."

If that be what it gonna take to git outta here, McLeary mused.

Once his laughing fit subsided, Powell took a puff and then waved his cigar around like a wand. "In all seriousness, McLeary," the planter said, his tone calm but curious, "you don't know much about this business, do you?"

"If by 'business'," McLeary answered, "you mean farmin' cotton, I reckon I know a thang or two. But if by 'business' you mean nigger-tradin', I know nothin' o' the sort."

"I was referring to the latter," Powell stated. "It's often referred to as the 'peculiar institution' these days."

"Peculiar, it be."

"It is, uh…" his voice trailed off. "Well, yes, I suppose 'peculiar' is an appropriate way to describe it. It is peculiar in more ways than one."

"How ye figure?"

Powell took a drag and exhaled slowly. The fumes wrapped him up in a fog of thick smoke.

"My grandfather," he began, his voice suddenly low and solemn, "worked on a ship that transported Africans to North America. He never spoke much of it; said it was ugly work. But the trade couldn't have been too hard on him because years later, he purchased this property, right here, and owned a few Negroes himself. Then my father built off of his work and bought a few more. The next thing you know, here I am, the third generation, living off quite a generous sum of money."

"That don' sound too bad, I suppose."

"On the surface," Powell continued, "it is a prosperous trade, if you have the know-how, of course. *However*… it is also an inherited trade, for better or worse. It is inherited by both the slave *and* the planter."

"What're you gettin' at, Henry?"

"The slave is born into bondage," he said. "He doesn't have a say one way or another about where he's going or what he's doing. The planter, should he come from a family of slaveholders, is born into a system in which he must constantly walk on shaky ground."

"How's that, ye reckon?"

"This institution," his voice sank to a whisper, "has faced opposition over the years, but never before has it been as strong as it is now. Take this Republican Party, for instance. They've created quite a ruckus, and I fear that if they take control of the White House, slave labor will be eradicated."

"You mean there be talk o' gettin' rid o' the instetution?"

Powell sighed and took another draw. "Not explicitly," he answered. "At least not yet. Lincoln says that if he's elected, all newly admitted states west of the Mississippi will be free states. Personally, I think he wants to outlaw slave labor in *all* states. It's a move that, dare he try it, will not be met with open arms. In fact, it will be met with armed resistance."

McLeary raised the cigar to his lips and exhaled slowly. He never took a liking to politics. To him, it was nothing more than a load of hogwash and empty promises. No party or candidate could convince him otherwise. Voting was a privilege that he never bothered to exercise, nor did he ever have any intention of doing so. As long as the sun shone on his world, that was all that mattered.

"The gall of that man," the planter fumed, "thinking that he can rob us of our rights. Does he not realize that southern plantations produce enough cotton to sustain the entire *world*? If he were to outlaw slave labor, the southern economy would be in ruins. The northern states would share in the same fate too. There is too much dependency on southern products for the northerners to put the noose around us. This union, fragile though it may be, has an economy that works like a machine. Without all the cogs working efficiently, we're *all* at a loss." Powell scowled and puffed away bitterly. "But I digress…"

McLeary paused before asking, "Ye think this Lincoln feller be winnin' this time 'round?"

The planter shook his head in disgust. He spoke dryly. "If you were to ask me that on the first of this year, I would've said you had a better chance of seeing this country fly under a Cherokee flag than you would of that man becoming president. But as the days pass, more and more states seem to be rallying behind the Republican Party… and I fear those battleground states may shift against us."

"Who knows," McLeary shrugged. "Never gave politics much thought, ye understan'."

"You're an old-timer through and through, McLeary," Powell acknowledged, "and for that you have my respect. You're the only man I know who can look the other way in every situation."

"It ain't hard if you have the mind to."

"Well," the planter laughed uneasily, "I suppose the old ways haven't been as lost on you as they have on me. Like you, I remember a much simpler time. A time when a man didn't have to worry about his property being taken away from him, or his rights being infringed upon. But our world's changing every day, and sooner or later it will catch up to us. It's not my place to tell you how to live your life, McLeary, but I would urge you to look out for yourself. If Lincoln has his way, I fear that all of Washington will be coming down upon us."

McLeary bit his tongue. Perhaps the planter's late-night antics had finally caught up with him. If he was worried about some sort of large-scale northern invasion, he was gravely mistaken. Sure, there were radicals out there, and although they were becoming increasingly vocal, their numbers were relatively few. The heart of the matter was simple: the North had a culture of its own, and so did the South. Neither side stood in the way of the other, and that was the way it was. He was sure of it. After all, that was the way he had always known it to be...

McLeary spoke up. "Henry," he said, "if I may be frank with ye, I be wantin' to know the meanin' of our visit. You ain't bad company or nothin', it just be that, er..."

Powell laughed. "No offense taken," he said. "Please forgive me, McLeary, sometimes these thoughts of mine twist and turn my head around so much that I forget the most basic things. As for the reason of your visit, it has to do with a little extravaganza that I'll be hosting on the Fourth of July. Some pals of mine will be coming up from Charleston to partake in an evening of food, drinks, and all sorts of mischief." Powell flashed him a grin. "Given that you are a man of such extraordinary talent," he continued, "the night would be amiss without some of your renowned cigars. I'll pay you a pretty penny for them too, and of course you and your wife are invited to attend and enjoy the evening."

McLeary fell silent for a moment. A little extra change in their pockets could go a long way. Perhaps he could treat Alice to another night out — they could have dinner, visit the theater, browse some of Richmond's high-end shops. He took little pleasure in venturing into the city, but if it made his wife happy, then it was worth it. "How much you reckon you'll be willin' to pay?"

"How does one hundred sound?"

"Sounds mighty fine to me."

"Would you be willing to make around several dozen of your little beauties?"

"Can do, sir."

"Wonderful!" Powell clasped his hands together. "Then we have ourselves a deal." He extended his hand and the two men shook on it.

At that moment, Rose stepped onto the porch and bowed her head politely. "Beg parden, Mas'r," she said. "Dinna be ready."

Powell flashed a smile towards his guest. "I hope you have an appetite, McLeary," he remarked, "because you and the Mrs. are in for a treat. My Negroes can cook with the best of them, and tonight you two will dine like royalty!"

McLeary wedged his cigar in between his lips and smiled. Perhaps the evening would not be so bad after all…

Chapter 4

Get ready, Herr Streicher, he told himself, *because tonight you are going to be the perfect gentleman.*

His reflection was foreign to him, but he liked what he saw nonetheless. With his back straight and shoulders cocked, he ran his hands along the trim of his navy-blue coat. Tucked beneath it were suspenders of the same color and a long white shirt. He studied his reflection from top to bottom, careful not to miss a single detail.

Dirty blonde hair, neatly combed and parted to one side. *Gut.* White handkerchief, properly folded and nestled in the coat pocket. *Gut.* Golden cufflinks. *Gut.* Brown shoes, freshly polished and laced. *Gut.* Everything was in order.

He cast himself one last glance. The suit was comfortable and tailored perfectly to his physique. There was nothing more he could have asked for, but still his smile faltered slightly. He was tall, lean… and yet perhaps he was a little too lean. The German diet eluded him, his father had always said with disdain. There needed to be more meat on his bones. Sure, he had the height of a man, but he was by no means a brawny fellow.

Streicher shook his head and turned away from the mirror. There was no time to doubt his appearance. He needed to concentrate his attention toward other matters. It was only a matter of minutes before the doors to the Hill residence would be thrown open, and all the city's elites would enjoy a night of good food and drinks. For Streicher, however, all the 'ballyhoo' that came with the evening — food, drinks, music, dancing — was insignificant. All that mattered was to be in the presence of a very special young woman, Emma Hill. Perhaps he would throw around a joke or two — as best as a German could — and get some laughs out of her. Or maybe he would offer his hand and together they would become the center of attention on the ballroom floor. Then, when the moon was full and glowing, he would swoop in for a kiss.

Of course, that was provided he made it to the end of the night without getting thrown out. Robert Hill, Emma's father, made the Germans seem like comedians. With a furrowed brow and lips that were fixed into a permanent scowl, Hill knew how to make even the toughest of men quiver in their boots. It must have been that unforgiving demeanor of his, Streicher concluded long ago, that brought his textile mill tremendous wealth. No one dared to displease him, and

Streicher refused to get on his bad side. If anything, the night was as much about impressing him as it was the girl of his dreams.

"My…" his mother's voice came from behind him. "You look very handsome, Erich."

Susanne Streicher, a dainty, petite woman with silver hair tucked in a bun, stood by the doorway at the far end of her son's room. With age, her bones grew frail, but she moved with the speed of a young person. Her light brown eyes and rosy cheeks filled every room she entered with warmth.

"Thank you, Mother." Streicher's smile resurfaced.

"Emma's a very lucky girl," she said. "To spend the night with you — I'm sure there are many other girls who would love to be in her place."

Streicher chuckled. "Well," he started, "here's hoping I can make it a special occasion for her. Do you think Father will…"

His mother waved a dismissive hand. "Don't listen to what he says," she advised him. "Go on and have a nice time tonight."

Streicher ventured downstairs and hurried towards the front door. Just as he curled his hand around the doorknob, a booming voice thundered from the end of the hallway.

"Boy!" his father called out. "Come here!" Streicher sighed as he backed away from the door and strolled slowly into the living room. It was a dimly lit and cramped space, and it reeked of aging mold and mildew. His father, Uwe Streicher, sat in a tattered armchair with a book in his lap. He was a large, burly man who spent his days hauling freight by the river. A lump forced its way into the young man's throat as his father met him with glaring eyes. "I don't want a scratch on that suit," he snapped at him. "Not. A. Scratch. Do you understand me?"

"Yes, sir."

"Mr. Gibbons was generous enough to let us rent it cheap for the night," his father rambled on, "and I don't want to throw away his business. Put it to good use and find yourself a nice Protestant girl."

The color fled Streicher's cheeks. His father would never approve if…

"Did you hear me, boy?" he questioned with dark, piercing eyes. "I said *Protestant* — not Catholic."

"Yes, sir," Streicher murmured. "But Emma invited…"

"Then break her heart if you have to," was the response. "Her family practically bathes in wealth; she'll have no trouble finding a suitor."

His father sat the book on a small table beside him and gripped each arm of the chair. Suddenly, his complexion began to redden. Streicher bit his lip; he should have fled the house when he had the chance.

"Twenty-three years old," his father started angrily, "and you still lack direction. I married your mother when I was eighteen, and we sailed to this country with nothing but the clothes on our backs. Day and night, I slaved away for you. It wasn't a generous living, but I did what I could to ensure that your future had more prospects than mine ever did. Yet here you stand now, a single man, who for too long has had his sights set on a girl who he will *never* marry. Time and time again, the men ask me, 'When's your boy getting married, Streicher'? Time and time again, I tell them, 'It's hard to say'… And they laugh and laugh. You are an embarrassment to me. *An embarrassment!* It's bad enough you spend your days churning out nigger-loving filth for some drunken Irish imbecile. Now you can't even find yourself a woman… Well, it all ends tonight. I'll permit you to go to that party, but you will find yourself a girl who your mother and I *approve* of. And I don't want to hear any excuses, boy. You *will* find yourself a girl, and by the end of the year, you *will* marry her. Understand?"

Streicher's throat was dry. It was as if he could barely breathe. As the stale air lingered around them, he had no choice but to comply. His father folded his arms and eyed him expectantly.

"Well?" he questioned. "Are you going to answer me, boy, or do I have to sit around and wait for you?"

"Sorry, sir…"

"Speak up!"

"Yes," Streicher's voice shook.

"Yes what?"

"Yes, sir, I promise that I will find a Protestant girl to marry."

His father stared at him long and hard with glaring eyes.

"Erich," his mother's gentle tone broke the silence. "You're running late. Get going and enjoy yourself, alright?"

The young man nodded and quickly started for the door. As he ventured out into the street and felt the cool summer breeze slap at his cheeks, he hurried away from the old house, not daring to look back.

***

There was something about a setting sun that calmed his spirit. His heartbeat slowed and his breathing relaxed. As he strode down the street, surrounded on both sides by towering brick buildings and piping factories, he reveled in the freedom. There was no authority to answer to — he was on his own. He did not have to please his father. He did not have to please Shane Doyle.

Doyle…

A grin spread across Streicher's lips.

His 'manifesto', or so the Irishman had called it, had been met with a rousing review earlier in the day. Doyle had praised him for declaring that the Fugitive Slave Acts were 'a black mark on America's legacy' that would 'fester like a disease' until southern planters could 'cure their heads of self-serving greed and wicked deeds'.

"You're a damn rebel, is what you are!" Doyle had proclaimed proudly. He had waved his paper around like a flag, as if to show the world that the *Freedom Fightin' Firebrands* were ready to throw a haymaker upon southern high society.

Such praise was welcomed by the young man, but by no means was he ready to march into the streets and declare himself a freedom fighter. It was his job to craft anything and everything that would make pro-slavery blood boil. At the end of the day, what mattered most was that money lined his pockets. In fact, as far as money was concerned, he benefited nicely.

He had saved up enough over the years to be able to afford an apartment of his own. The only barrier that prevented him from making such an investment was that he had yet to marry a certain someone…

Streicher shook his head.

Who was his father to say who he could or could not marry? And why did it matter if he was Protestant and Emma was Catholic? They both shared feelings for each other, and that was far more important than anything else.

There was a way of the old country, a certain set of customs and traditions, that he never could quite understand. He may have descended from German blood, but he was born in Philadelphia. His parents may have come from the Old World, but he knew only the new one. Yet even in the New World, it seemed that every person had a strict allegiance to the old ways…

The Protestants married the Protestants. The Catholics married the Catholics. The rich married the rich. The poor married the poor. So on and so forth…

He bit his lip.

Maybe it was not him at all, like his father had always made it seem. Maybe the world was simply too stubborn and unchanging. Maybe, dare he even think of it, the world needed more Shane Doyles. Someone who could stand up for change and make everyone question their values and ways of life.

Then again…

He was not looking for some drastic phenomenon. If anything, his desire was quite simple: to live comfortably and one day raise a family with Emma Hill. Why his father made it so difficult for him to achieve his dream, he would never know…

A shrill jingle rang out and interrupted his thoughts. He gazed upon a crowded street corner, where men gathered around to hear some fellow who propped himself upon a soapbox. With a tri-cornered hat and decorated blue jacket, his outfit resembled the uniform that men wore in the days of the Revolution. He waved a small bell in his hand.

"Sons of liberty," he called out to the crowd. "Hear this message, and hear it well. Our blessed union is on the verge of *collapse*! As November approaches, we must be ready to answer once and for all the burning question that our forefathers put forth years ago… Are *all* men created equal? Our liberties are tender and fragile, threatened by southern interests and unruly states whose lust for power know no end. Hear me, Philadelphia — the birthplace of American independence — and hear me well. We need a strong, unbreakable *union* to counter southern aggression. We need an unwavering *federal* system that will keep states in check."

Several cheers and whistles erupted from the crowd as men huddled together and yelled out with glee.

"Hear! Hear!"

"God bless the Union!"

"Down with southern rights!"

"I humbly ask of all of you," the self-proclaimed patriot continued, "that when the time comes for you to cast your ballot, vote for the *only* man who is fit for the job... Honest Abe Lincoln!"

Thunderous applause.

"Hooray for Ol' Abe!"

"Lincoln for president!"

"Elect a Republican president!"

Streicher shook his head as he strode past the rambunctious crowd. Shane Doyle must have been buried in there somewhere, screeching and screaming among the rest of them. He was certain of it.

How could they get themselves all riled up when the election was five months away? Did none of them have wives to get home to, or families to take care of? Whatever the case, it did not matter in the least to him.

The night was still very young, and there was a beautiful woman waiting for him...

The Hill family owned a generous estate tucked away on the outskirts of the city. A long, winding cobblestone driveway led the way to a four-story brick mansion. Polished windows glistened in the gentle sunlight along the exterior. A lush, sprawling lawn surrounded the mansion; finely trimmed bushes and ferns lined the driveway towards the main entrance. Horse-drawn carriages of all shapes and sizes made their way in a parade-like fashion towards a set of large wooden doors.

As Streicher strolled along the edge of the driveway, careful not to get trampled by the stampede that passed him by, his breath grew short. Greeting the guests was the stern-eyed, no-nonsense man known as Robert Hill. With dark, beady eyes and a crescent nose, he resembled a vulture more than anything else... or so Streicher believed. He was a tall, lanky fellow, not particularly toned or well-built, but his sharp gaze made up for any lack of imposing physical qualities.

Streicher drew nearer, and as those black beads narrowed and drew their sights upon him, his palms became cold and clammy. His legs stiffened. The young man nodded politely in his direction and offered a weak smile. As the two of them stood before each other, Hill's lips tightened.

The German cleared his throat and extended his hand. "G-Good evening, Mr. Hill," he stammered. "It is a pleasure, sir…"

Hill ignored his gesture and folded his arms. A lump found its way into Streicher's throat.

I should never have come, he thought miserably.

"I am p-pleased to see you again. Sir." Streicher fumbled.

Again, he was met with silence. Black holes bore into him, assessing his every fear and worry. A faint layer of sweat coated his brow. What had once been a cool, refreshing summer night suddenly felt like an oven…

"Streicher," Hill stated flatly.

The young man lowered his hand slowly. "Emma…"

"She's inside." The older gentleman stood guard in front of the doorway. "Are you still involved with that good-for-nothing heap of vermin who goes by the name of Shane Doyle?"

The blood fled Streicher's cheeks.

"Well, I…"

"Answer me, boy — yes or no."

"Yes, sir."

A dizzying spell overcame Streicher. It was not so much a reaction that worried him as it was a lack of one.

Sure enough, Hill remained like a statue. Entirely frozen and unflinching, as if nothing had happened. Then, his icy tone bit the air. "Why?" he demanded.

"It pays well, sir."

"Is that so?"

"Yes, sir."

"So, you find it acceptable," Hill questioned further, "to work for a man who accuses my industry of operating like a 'human slaughterhouse', in which all profits fill the pockets of 'scoundrels, their whores, and the like'?"

Streicher was at a loss for words. "Sir, you must understand that my interest in Mr. Doyle's pursuits is strictly a professional one," he said.

"There is nothing *professional* about his business, that much I can assure you."

"Please understand, sir," Streicher tried again, "that I am in it solely for a paycheck. Nothing more."

"Yet you fuel his fires." Hill shook his head. "Streicher, you better look like you are ready to turn things around."

"Of course, sir."

"If you say that you do not align yourself with Doyle's 'agenda', as we'll put it," Hill continued, his voice firm and steady, "then who, dare I ask, will you support in the upcoming election?"

Streicher's mind became frantic. Day in and day out, he was thrown into a political frenzy. He had to know the names of the candidates, their stances, what party they were affiliated with… and yet his mind drew a blank. *For God's sake, think,* he pleaded to himself. *Come on, think of a name! Any name!*

"Douglas!" he called out, perhaps a little louder than he may have wished. "Stephen Douglas."

Hill nodded his head slowly, deep in thought. The young man held his breath. He was unsure whether to be relieved or terrified.

"Douglas, eh?" The sharp-eyed gentleman mulled it over. "A moderate candidate. More level-headed than Lincoln, I'll give you that. Yet I fear that those debates he held with Lincoln did not fare well for him. Do you agree?"

"I do, sir," Streicher quickly replied. He would have agreed to anything if it would please the man who stood before him.

"John Bell is the better choice," the other insisted. "Given that he owns Negroes himself, he recognizes the plight that many planters are facing today. If there is nothing to drive the southern economy, then the northern economy will collapse as well. It is unfortunate that Lincoln and his… *hell-raisers*, shall we say, seem to ignore this fact."

"Very unfortunate, indeed," Streicher went along. "I take it you have an interest in such matters?"

"When you're the rightful owner of a textile mill, you have a *vested* interest in a great many things."

"I understand, sir."

Hill's probing eyes remained locked upon him. "I suppose there's no use beating around the bush any longer," the older gentleman started. "You are here to see my daughter, are you not?"

"I am, sir."

Hill took a step towards him. A fire burned in him, Streicher was sure of it, and it was longing to spread. Despite Emma's gracious intentions, perhaps it was for the better if he had declined her invitation. "Listen to me carefully, boy," Hill said, his voice lowering to a harsh whisper. "Understand?"

"Yes, sir."

"She's very fond you," he stated, "but I'm sure you already know that. She speaks of you often — a little *too* often for my liking, but I listen anyway. When I told her about this party, the first sentence that spilled out of her mouth was that she wanted to invite you."

Streicher tried hard not to crack a smile. "I'm flattered, sir…" he admitted honestly.

"You must understand," Hill continued, "that I love my little girl more than anything, and it is for that reason and that reason only that I complied with her request. But before you walk through these doors, know this and know it well: you two are *only* to remain friends. Nothing more. Do you hear me?"

"Loud and clear, sir."

"Good," Hill nodded. "Don't try any funny business while you're in there either. And know that two eyes will be following you like a hawk… *at all times*."

"Of course… sir."

"Show yourself in."

"Certainly, sir," Streicher nodded and hurried past him. "Thank you."

As the wooden doors closed tightly behind him, Streicher let out a long breath and frantically searched the room for a tall glass of water.

Yet another rousing conversation with Mr. Hill.

***

The grand ballroom was spacious and comfortable. Finished with freshly painted white walls and a polished hardwood floor, guests milled about the room with ease and marveled at the plush furnishings and fine antiques. Servants bustled about one way and another, tending to empty glasses and requests for hors d'oeuvres.

Streicher stood in the middle of the room, pale-faced and coated in sweat, holding a glass of water in his trembling hand. At least the hard part was behind him, or so he hoped…

He scanned the room eagerly for the only person who mattered tonight. As men and women passed him by, dressed elegantly in their finest attire, his search was fruitless.

Suddenly, a cheerful voice came from behind him. "Erich!"

He turned around and saw the blonde-haired young woman, whose curls bounced gently with every step she took. Fair-skinned and slim-shouldered, her delicate frame seemed to glide across the floor. She wore a light blue dress, which matched the gentle glow of her eyes. There was a calm, soothing aura about her that made the young man's legs grow numb and his heart skip a beat. With her long eyelashes, finely curled, and lips polished red, it took everything in his power not to sweep her up into his arms.

Emma stepped towards him, arms extended, but then she recoiled slightly and offered her hand instead. He kissed it, and her radiant smile grew wide.

"To tell you the truth," she began, "I was beginning to think you weren't coming."

Streicher returned the smile. "If it means seeing you, Emma," he said, "you better believe I'll be here. If I have to shlep through rain, snow, or a full-blown, guns-popping riot to get here, then that's what it takes."

She laughed. "Well, at the very least, let's pray that the third one doesn't happen any time soon."

Streicher winked and raised his glass. "Amen."

Before he knew it, Emma reached for his hand and began escorting him towards the rear of the ballroom. He faltered slightly and became tangled by his own feet, which nearly caused the water to escape from his glass. With wide, frantic eyes, he snapped his head around and saw that the main doors remained closed. In all likelihood, Emma's father was still posted out front, awaiting any stragglers with a cold stare. Still, the young man held his breath as they strolled through a set of rear doors and out onto a small balcony.

The sky bathed in purple as the sun dipped below the horizon. A soft breeze brushed up against them, and for the first time that night, Streicher felt entirely at ease.

They were alone, overlooking a lush yard decorated by trimmed shrubs and blooming flowers.

Emma turned to face him and flashed her beaming smile. It was truly incredible, Streicher could not deny, that in the two and a half years he had known her, she had not changed a bit. They had met outside a bakery, of all places, on a frigid, rainy February morning. It had been particularly crowded that morning, and a long line had formed outside the shop. Emma had stood in front of him, and a friendly wink here and a wide smile there sparked an instant bond between them.

She was a year younger than him, and yet her maturity reached far beyond her years. Having been sent off to boarding school for four years, she had learned reading and arithmetic at a very young age. Eloquent and polished, her keen abilities led her to become a highly intelligent and free-thinking young woman.

In the time they had known one another, they had visited each other sparingly. If it were not for his father's religious intolerance and her father's stringent standards, Streicher would have seen to it that every day was spent with her.

Streicher shook his head and cast a glance towards the twinkling sky. Why did his father have to be the one who decided when his time with Emma was up?

No, he thought angrily. *I'm in control of my situation, whether he wants me to be or not*. His father's stubbornness was his greatest foe. To the contrary, there was no quarrel to be had with his mother, who had welcomed Emma to their home with open arms. Each time the two of them had crossed paths, they would share tea together and strike up a whirlwind of conversation about one thing or another.

As for Emma's mother, however, he had never been given the opportunity to meet her. She had passed away from cholera when Emma was a little girl. Perhaps that was why her father was such a bitter man, Streicher often wondered. Nonetheless, Emma spoke fondly of the memories she had of her mother, and it was for that reason that he was inclined to believe that she would have approved of the two of them being together.

His thoughts were interrupted as Emma leaned against him, her head resting upon his shoulder. He sat his glass upon the rail and wrapped her in his arms. Her baby blue eyes sparkled in the fading light. She gazed upwards at him, her lips pressed tightly and her eyes suddenly filled with concern.

"What's wrong?" she asked softly.

He tried his best to remain calm. "Nothing," he murmured. "Why do you ask?"

"Erich, you know me better than this," she replied. "I can tell when there's something troubling you. What is it?"

Streicher grew silent.

"It wasn't my father, was it?" she laughed nervously. "I hope he wasn't too hard on you."

"It wasn't..." Well, not entirely...

"What's the problem then?" she tried again and placed her hand on his cheek. "You can tell me."

He breathed slowly, gazed upon her with sympathetic eyes, and spoke softly. "I've been looking forward to this day ever since you told me about it. It's been all I could think about for weeks. But before I left tonight, my father told me that…"

His words fled him. A tense silence followed, and all Emma could do was nod and lower her gaze to the floor. She blinked once, twice, and then her eyes grew tearful. Slowly, steadily, they streamed down her cheeks. "Say no more," she choked out. "I know…"

Streicher felt helpless as he held her in his arms. The urge to speak, to provide comforting words, was lost upon him, and he fought desperately to suppress his own tears.

His mind raced. There *had* to be an alternative. Their relationship was precious, and there was no way he would allow it to be ended by anybody. One way or another, he would see to it that they remained together. As his thoughts grew clearer, there appeared to be only one solution. A solution that had for so long brought about many restless nights…

"Emma," he said, "let's run away and get married."

Her gaze remained locked to the floor, where she stood silent and unmoving. Lost in thought, a sea of emotions… "What?" she whispered.

He placed a finger under her jaw and delicately raised her chin. Heavy, tear-filled eyes stared at him, but there was a spark in them that had not been there only moments ago. A speck of hope…

"Emma," he began gently, "I want you to be my wife. I'm sorry that this is such a poor attempt at a proposal, but I don't want to lose you. I don't want to lose what we have. What do you say?"

A smile resurfaced upon her lips. Tears continued to flow down her cheeks, but she let out a cry of joy. "Yes," she nodded excitedly. "My answer's yes…"

Now it was Streicher's turn to smile. He leaned towards her and planted a kiss on her lips. They stood still, heads together, not caring about anything else in the world. They had each other, and they would be together until the end of their days.

"Run away, you say?" Emma asked. "To where?"

"Somewhere," Streicher answered, "where it's the two of us. *Only* the two of us…"

"You're sure about this?"

He nodded. "I'll figure it out," he assured her. "Don't worry about a thing, alright? We'll get married, have a place of our own, and raise a family together. How does that sound?"

"Perfect," she said, gasping. "Absolutely perfect."

His smile grew wider. As he tightened his hold of her, he was lost in a world of delight. The future, with all its uncertainties, no longer seemed quite so daunting. He would find a place for them tucked away in the countryside somewhere.. Away from a world that was becoming increasingly divided and bitter with each passing day. He would find a simple job where he could leave his mind at ease and return home for dinner each night. A simple life came with certain privileges that were invaluable. In time, all would be made right…

Suddenly, the rear door was thrown open and a gruff voice sounded off. "Hands off my daughter!"

Streicher quickly complied and stepped away from Emma.

"Father…"

"I don't want to hear it," he fired at her. "Emma, get inside."

"But…"

"Now!"

Emma gave Streicher a pitiful glance and then made her way into the ballroom.

With eyes that boiled with rage, Hill stormed over to him. Just as it seemed as if he was about to send him to the floor, he stopped dead in his tracks and scowled. "Before I do something I'll regret," Hill's voice shook, "it'd be for the best that you show yourself out of here."

"Certainly, sir."

"From now on," he declared, "you two are no longer permitted to see each other. This has gone on for long enough, and I will tolerate it no further. My daughter will marry a respectable man, not some low-life who spends his time spewing controversy. Do I make myself clear?"

"Yes, sir."

"Get going then," he demanded. "I'll be watching you."

Streicher nodded and made his way back into the ballroom with Hill trailing closely behind. As he meandered through swarms of anonymous faces, he spotted Emma seated in a chair in the corner of the room. Her eyes glistened in the gentle light, and as she saw him, those blue gems grew wide.

"I'll write to you," he mouthed to her.

She nodded slowly, and the corner of her lips raised ever so slightly. It had been a splendid occasion, albeit a speedy one. As Streicher barreled through the front doors and strolled down the driveway, he could not help but smile.

He would return home immediately. There were many things to attend to, and many preparations needed to be made. A future needed to be mapped out and protected. With hope on his side, he would get started right away. Perhaps the evening would not be so bad after all...

Chapter 5

McLeary's mind was at ease. He sat at the kitchen table, sleeves rolled up to his elbows, and went about his business rolling dried tobacco leaves into cigars.

It was a grim afternoon, with heavy rains and raging thunder. Unrelenting hisses and roaring pops sounded off above the quaint little log cabin, but he paid it no mind. There was a job to be done, and any man worthy of his craft would see to it that it was done well. Powell had asked for several dozen cigars, and in a matter of days, he would have them. Two weeks of baking under a scorching sun had provided the savvy farmer with more than enough dried leaves. With any luck, he would have enough left over to create a respectable stash of his own. After all, a good day was not possible without enjoying two or three cigars.

Alice sat in a rocking chair in a corner of the room and studied his ever-growing pile. There was too much ruckus for her to enjoy a good book. Not that it mattered to her anyway — every now and then a good storm was welcomed. Listening to the tap of the rain perked up her ears and made her heart relax.

She took a deep breath and folded her hands in her lap. How funny it was that her husband could never quite give up his craft. More than anyone, she knew that it was a hobby for him as much as it had been a profession. As long as he still found pleasure in it, that was all that mattered.

She smiled. "Almost finished?"

"Nearly there, darlin'," he mumbled, eyes concentrated upon his work. "Won' be long now till Powell 'n' his boys have at 'em."

"Good." She nodded and then added with a smirk, "So where will you be taking me once you get paid?"

McLeary glanced up at her and grinned. "That depends," he answered. "Where you got yer heart set on goin'?"

"How about the theater? We could have dinner beforehand."

"How'd I know you was gonna say that?"

"After forty-five years of marriage," she said, "I reckon you ought to know me like the back of your hand."

McLeary nodded. "I s'ppose so."

A calm silence lingered as Alice gazed out at the grey sky. Sheets of rain pelted the side of their cabin, and she listened as the wind whipped around them.

She spoke up. "How much longer do you think this storm will last, Thomas?"

A faint grunt was heard from the other room. She took that as, "I don't know."

Silence.

"Thomas," she called out.

"Hmm?"

"About that payment from Henry Powell," she began, "have you given it more thought about purchasing an extra hand to help out around here?"

The old farmer looked up from his work and frowned. "There ain't no thought to give," he said. "We ain't gettin' a hand."

"But don't you think it might be a worthwhile investment? I'm sure Henry wouldn't mind offering some suggestions as to how to go about it…"

"I thought you be wantin' to go to the theater, Alice."

"Well, yes," she said, "but it might be in our best interests to look out for ourselves and get a Negro of our own."

"*I'll* decide what be our best interests," McLeary stated. "We talked 'bout this before. We's fine on our own, understan'?"

"But you saw how it is over at Henry's place," she protested. "They cook for him, clean for him, tend to his crops… We're not getting any younger. If we have the means, it would be wise to…"

"I said no!"

"Why not?"

"Don' question me, woman."

"All I asked was…"

"It don' sit well with me."

"What do you mean?" she asked. "Many people own slaves."

"That don' mean *we* gotta."

"You're looking at this the wrong way," she insisted. "If we purchased a Negro, I wouldn't let the poor thing wither away. I'd care for it as if it was my child."

"Yer child, ya say?" the farmer raised an eyebrow. "What be yer plan if this child o' yours got on up one day 'n' run off somewheres?"

"That wouldn't happen."

"Anythin' can happen, Alice," he said. "Think back on that bad business some time ago down 'n Southampton County. Don' you remember?"

How could she forget?

It had been nearly thirty years since an army of Negroes massacred scores of white men, women, and children. Word had spread rapidly of the uprising, and there were whispers that as far down as Alabama, slaves were banding together and overthrowing their masters. It had been a panic, plain and simple, and the rebels were routed in a matter of days. Even so, she could not forget the restless nights that came in the immediate aftermath.

The McLearys had spent five nights in their cellar, armed with a rifle that they kept beside their bed. Perhaps it had been an overreaction, she later thought, but the fear was real. Of course, it was figured that the number of Negroes who were killed in retribution more than tripled the number of white lives lost. But it was better to deter any troublemakers, Alice believed, than to have such a tragedy unfold again.

"Yes," she answered softly. "That I will never forget."

"I reckon Powell ain't sleepin' too good in them days."

"Probably not."

"This 'peculiar instetution'," her husband began, "be a very *dangerous* one. I don' want nothin' te do with it, and that be the final word. Understan'?"

Alice nodded.

A streak of lightning flashed across the horizon and lit up their cabin. The hairs on her skin stood up; there was something about the power of nature that left one speechless and humbled. She cast a glance towards her husband, who resumed his work without a care in the world. If lightning tore through the roof of their house, he would not even flinch. As he grew older, he seemed to become more and more wrapped up in his own world.

Then something caught her eye.

Behind her husband was a large window that overlooked their rear porch and tobacco farm. Tucked away on the far end of their property was an old barn, where McLeary stored all his tools for the harvesting season. He kept it safely secured at all times, but the door had come loose and swayed violently in the wind.

71

"Thomas," she said, "have a look behind you. The barn door is open."

McLeary paused from his work and shot a glance over his shoulder. The sight brought him abruptly to his feet, and he fetched his hat and hurried towards the rear door.

"Don't tell me you're going out there now," Alice pleaded with him. "Can't you wait until the storm passes?"

"It ain't lookin' like it be endin' soon," he muttered. "I don' want no critters runnin' 'round in there."

"You made sure the latch was shut this morning, didn't you?"

"I did," the farmer answered and placed a hand on the doorknob, ready to embrace the elements. "This sunnovagun musta blown it open."

"Be careful out there."

"Don' worry, hon," he assured her. "I ain't gonna be long."

Releasing a deep breath, he threw the door open and ran out into the raging storm.

***

He ran as fast as his legs could carry him. Each step sent mud flying in all directions, and his overalls were smeared in brown. Icy droplets pelted him from above and sent bitter chills down his spine. Through the sheets of rain, he strained his eyes and kept them trained upon the old barn.

It was not much longer until he splashed his way through the marshy field and hurried through the doorway. With the wind fighting against him, he struggled mightily to grab the door and fasten it shut behind him. Bent over and panting heavily, the old farmer carefully surveyed the flimsy wooden structure. Several of his rakes and hoes lay scattered across the floor.

Damn storm don' let up, he thought to himself as he collected his tools and propped them up against the wall. Just as he reached for the door handle to head back out, a faint rustling came to his ears. He paused. It was a low scratching sound coming from the far-right corner. The farmer shook his head. *Damn vermin…*

As he headed slowly towards the back, his boots crunching on old straw, dark shadows danced around him. Back and forth, they darted past him and disrupted his sight. Then, as he grew closer, the scratching ceased. Like an old watchdog, he narrowed his eyes and crept forward cautiously. There was something back there. Past stacks of old boxes and rusty tools, a form began to take shape…

Closer and closer, he ventured forth. The shadows began to lose their tricks, and his sight became clearer. When he cast his gaze upon the corner, his eyes grew wide and he nearly fell to the floor…

Trembling brown eyes stared back at him. She was a young woman, dark-skinned and thin, and she sat pressed against the wall with her knees to her chest. She wore a faded pink dress that was tattered and smeared in dark streaks. Wrapped around her head was a white cloth, and strands of sleek black hair dangled above her brow. Her skin glistened in the pale light, and beneath where she sat was a large puddle. There was a strange aura about her, which made the old farmer's breath grow short. Her jaw slackened, and as her mouth hung open, McLeary was unsure whether she would let out a guttural cry or fall faint upon the floor. Then something else caught his eye…

Dark splotches ran along her wrists and forearms. Before he could get a closer look at them, she quickly buried her arms in her lap.

McLeary stood with his hands on his hips, unable to utter a word, unable to comprehend the situation before him. Howling wind lashed at the walls and the rain hissed, but he gave it no thought. He stared at her, as if in a silent trance. Time stood still for what felt like an eternity, but then he spoke up.

"Got yerself in a bit o' trouble, ain't ye?" the farmer asked. "Ye picked a devil o' a time to go on 'n' run off."

She remained still and silent.

"Ye got a name?"

Those brown eyes stared at him, lost in a world of terror and uncertainty.

"Ye ain't mute?"

74

She shook her head slowly.

"Go on then," McLeary tried again, careful not to lose his patience. "Gimme yer name."

Thunder rumbled above them.

Her eyes twinkled in the darkness, and streams of tears rolled down her cheeks. She looked down at the floor and closed her eyes. "Betty," she answered softly.

"Betty," the farmer repeated, nodding his head. "Why you runnin' off, Betty?"

Suddenly, she let out a cry and buried her head in her arms. Heavy sobs echoed off the walls.

McLeary sighed and rested his arms at his sides. With small, careful steps, he approached her and knelt to meet her gaze. "Listen here, Betty." He spoke calmly. "Look at me, hon…"

Slowly, she raised her tear-stained face and met his eyes. Something haunted the young woman; McLeary saw it plainly. Her panicked, bloodshot gaze made his skin crawl. One way or another, she had seen an ugly side of life. What had happened to her exactly, one could only wager a guess. McLeary's reluctance to push for answers was strong, but if he did not get something out of her, someone else most certainly would. And the Lord only knew if their methods would be as gentle as his…

"Now," the farmer began, "how 'bout you tell me where ye from?"

She shook her head.

"Betty," he tried once more, "I be a good man, ye understan'? I ain't gonna hurt ye. But ye's gotta tell me where ye from so I can get ye back to ye master."

"If ya be da good man ya say ya is," Betty whispered, "den ya ain't gonna take me back der."

"Well, we gotta figure somethin' out," McLeary stated, "cause ya ain't livin' here."

"Why na?"

"Why not?" the farmer repeated, startled by such a response. He raised an eyebrow. "You 'n' me both know why we can' do that. I's bound by law, ye understan', to return ye to ye owner."

"Please don'!"

"He ain't kind to ye, be that it?" he asked. "I's seen he gave ya a good bruisin'."

"Mas'r says I be a bad nigga." She spoke bitterly. "I don' work gooda dan dem rest in de fields. I's lazy, he say."

"That be true, Betty?" was the question. "You ain't workin' hard nuff?"

"I don' owe him nothin'," she growled. "*He* took me 'way from ma child. *He* took ma world 'way from me."

"So ya figered ya gone lookin' for this child o' yours?"

She nodded as more tears ran down her cheeks.

"Well now," McLeary sighed. "Where ya reckon this child be?"

"Somewheres in Georgia," she said sadly, "but dat be some time ago. He coulda been sold 'way from his first mas'r."

"May be." McLeary nodded. "Betty, I can' promise ye nothin' if I turn my head 'n' let ye on yer way. But what I *can* promise ye is that if ye get yerself caught down a ways, they's likin' to be less fergivin' than me."

"I ain't gonna get caught."

"Ye keep yerself cooped up where you ain't s'pposed to," the farmer warned, "I reckon ye will."

She shook her head and cast a heavy, defeated glance towards the floor. "I ain't afraid o' dyin', suh," she whispered. "They's took everythin' from me. Wuh more can I lose?"

The old farmer bit his lip. There was nothing he could say that would compel her to abandon her cause. Not that it mattered much, of course. Her fate lay in his hands…

He let out a sigh and propped himself up to his feet. A strand of rope resting on a box beside them caught his attention. He grabbed it and coiled it through his fingers.

"Betty." McLeary spoke softly. "I don' wanna ask ye again. Tell me where ya's from…"

As she raised her head in his direction, those brown fires that had blazed in her eyes were extinguished. They lingered in a dreary haze, and she appeared to grow numb to her surroundings. Without a word, she offered her wrists to him.

"Betty…"

77

"Powell plan'ation."

Lord almighty, McLeary thought as he tied the rope around her wrists. He brought her to her feet and began to escort her towards the door. "I hope ye can fergive me," he said. "I don' take no pleasure in this…"

"It don' mattuh none," she responded quietly. "Long as I be livin', I's gonna go out 'gain 'n' 'gain."

"I'll tell ya, Betty," McLeary said, nodding, "that don' surprise me the least…"

The farmer threw open the door, and the two of them hurried out into the storm.

***

The trek to Powell's place had been as McLeary expected it would be: wet and miserable. Several times along the way he had to give the young woman a gentle shove to keep her feet moving at a steady pace. Even so, such efforts had done little to motivate her. Betty sauntered along with her shoulders dipped and her head hung low. She paid the rain and thunder no mind. It was true then, McLeary figured. She was a defeated soul…

They stood beneath the awning of the palace, clothes soaked and dripping from head to toe. McLeary pounded at the door and before long, it swung open and a grim-faced Rose greeted them.

"Oh my…" she gasped. "Do come in, Missuh MucLeary. I be gettin' de mas'r for ya."

McLeary remained where he stood. All that mattered was returning home as quickly as possible and putting on a fresh change of clothes. Before long, Powell rushed over to them with flushed cheeks and wide eyes. Rose and Sampson trailed behind him. It was as if all activity within the place suddenly ceased, and all eyes were trained on what was about to unfold…

"God be praised," the planter said, sighing. "McLeary, I am forever in your debt. She's been missing for over a day now." Powell glanced behind him and gestured for Sampson to approach. "Take Betty here for me," he ordered. "See to it that she is disciplined accordingly…"

The boy nodded and escorted her into the house. Once she disappeared from sight, a lump found its way into the farmer's throat. His intentions, though they were lawful and well-meaning, would not bring about such a pleasant outcome for her…

"I do apologize, McLeary," the planter said. "Bringing all of this trouble upon you was not my intention."

The farmer waved a hand. "Don' worry none, Henry," he muttered. "It be all over now…"

"Well, please understand, good sir," Powell began, "that this act of yours is not taken lightly. I will compensate you for your trouble, and that's a promise. Now, please come in, will you? We can get a fire going and get you warmed up. I'll see to it that you get a fresh change of clothes as well. Would you care for something to eat? Or a drink, perhaps?"

McLeary shook his head. "No, thanks," he politely refused. "I reckon it be for the best if I git goin'."

"Are you sure?"

"Yessir."

"Let me arrange a carriage…"

"No need to, Henry."

"McLeary, don't be foolish. It's pouring…"

"Please," the farmer insisted. "I got here by foot 'n' so's I can go back by foot."

"If you wish," Powell remarked dryly. "At the very least, let me see you off…"

The planter stepped onto the porch and shut the door behind him. Heavy rain tapped above them as they stood facing each other. Heavy, bloodshot eyes met the farmer's gaze. Powell folded his arms and began to speak. "Before you think otherwise," his voice was low and solemn, "know that I am a good man, McLeary. A good, honest, by-the-book kind of man."

"I ain't sayin' you isn't, Henry."

"The look on your face says different. I am a man who prides himself on his reputation, and I will not tolerate any notion or suggestion that is detrimental towards it."

His words sent a jolt down McLeary's spine. "Gee, Henry," he said. "I's sorry if I upset ye. Ain't meanin' to, ye understan'."

"I've been in this business far longer than anyone else in Shady Grove," he divulged, "and this is the *first* time any of my hands ran off on me."

"You's only human, Henry." The farmer tried to reassure him. "You ain't gonna know when somethin' like this gonna happen till it do. There be nothin' the matter now. Everythin' be taken care of."

"It's bad business," Powell sulked, "if this sort of thing happens. I pride myself in the way I treat my Negroes. They're clothed, fed, sheltered — anything they could possibly need is here for them. Granted, I run a tight ship... but you need to in order to survive in this business. They don't come cheap, and I don't pay for them to sit around. They do what I tell them to, and they work until I tell them they are finished. Betty, forgive her soul, is the only one who doesn't seem to understand the way things work around here. Then again, I reckon she *does*; she simply refuses to do her work."

"She be speakin' 'bout this child o' hers," McLeary said. "Ye know a thang or two 'bout that?"

The planter nodded his head slowly, his thoughts drawn back to a tragic memory. "The Mrs and I were down in Atlanta a few years back," he began, "and she took a liking to Betty. I said to my wife, 'Why don't you get yourself some jewelry or a nice dress instead?' but she wouldn't have it. Tearing a mother from her child is ugly business, and it's not something I took pleasure in. But her son — I reckon he was four or five years old at the time — was fetching a good sum, and I didn't have

81

the money to purchase them together. Next thing you know, the poor girl's screeching and screaming 'Bloody murder!' and this and that. From the moment we bought her, I had a bad feeling that she was going to be trouble."

"Well, Henry," McLeary said, "I reckon she be wantin' her freedom. Wantin' to go down 'n' find her son."

Powell laughed nervously. "You don't think it's crossed my mind about giving it to her?" he muttered. "It'd certainly save me a few hours of tossing and turning each night, that much I can tell you."

"Why don' ye then?"

"It's not that easy," he stated. "What's she have to her name besides the clothes on her back? Nothing. She would go down there and someone would snatch her up and sell her off for a good price."

"I s'ppose ye be right."

"She wouldn't have it any easier up north," Powell continued, "for as much as the abolitionists would like you to believe. Take a trip up to one of the factories in Boston or Philadelphia. Those workers are up from sunrise to sunset, slaving away in darkness until they keel over, and for what? Breadcrumbs? And they're *white* workers, mind you. I find it hard to believe that a Negro, much less a Negro woman, would be spared from such conditions."

"Ain't likely," McLeary agreed. "But I caught a gander o' her arms 'n' wrists. It don' look like she be benefittin' much stayin' round here, if it ain't too bold o' me to say."

"I believe, sir," the planter said defensively, "that *is* too bold for my liking. How I handle my Negroes is *my* business, and mine alone."

"Sorry, Henry."

"Don't make a devil out of me, alright?" he warned. "Like I said, I run a tight ship. I am fair but firm, you see, and I do not tolerate any… *dissenters*, shall we say. 'You are here to work,' I tell them. 'Do what is asked of you and there will be no trouble. If you should refuse your work, then you will bear the consequences.' That's the trouble with Betty, I'm afraid. *If* she does her work — and that's a big 'if' — she does it without purpose. It's a shame that that business down in Georgia made her such a bitter soul. I pity the girl, really, I do… but it doesn't do me any good if she's throwing fits. If I give her special treatment, what message does that send to the rest of them? Sometimes it takes a good whack or two to get the point across, but that's the nature of the business. If there is money to be made, you can be assured that I will waste no time in making it."

McLeary shoved his hands into his pockets. As the planter carried on more and more about the so-called 'peculiar institution,' he found there to be nothing 'peculiar' about it at all. Two words summed up the business for what it was — bad and ugly. There was nothing good-natured or righteous about it, as much as Powell liked to believe. Not that he would tell him otherwise, of course. There were too many strong feelings tied into the matter.

"Forgive me, McLeary." The planter glanced at the floor. "I didn't mean to snap at you like that. These discussions can get so…"

"Say nothin' more, Henry," McLeary calmly interrupted. "I understan' where you's comin' from."

Powell bit his lip as his sorrowful gaze met the farmer. "Anymore," he said softly, "I feel like there's no winning. The press sets out to paint the southern planter as Satan himself, and then there's Lincoln with his rhetoric, which stokes the fire even more. Do forgive me if I am repeating myself, but as far as this institution is concerned, there is no talk about the *expansion* of slavery. There is only talk about the *existence* of it, and mark my words, its days are numbered if there is no action to be taken… Then again, I often wonder what difference it would make even if the country didn't bat an eye on the subject. One machine can match the work of a hundred hands, and I often wonder — for as much as I hate to admit it — if it's only a matter of time before slave labor is rendered obsolete. But therein lies a question… What shall become of the Negro then? He has no education. He has no standing in society. He would perform menial work, just as he's always done. That is the great dilemma of our time, you see, and I fear that these radical groups lack such vision. At least on the plantation, though it be a lowly existence, there is a place for him."

84

Powell shook his head and chuckled to himself. "There I go again." He offered a half-smile. "Pardon me, McLeary. Oftentimes I can't keep this trapper of mine shut."

The farmer returned a smile, albeit a forced one. "Don' worry none," he said for what felt like the thousandth time. "If you 'scuse me, I best be goin'. Don' want the wife to be waitin' up on me…"

"Of course," Powell remarked. "Are you sure you wouldn't like a ride back to your place? It's still coming down pretty hard…"

McLeary waved a hand. "Naw," he replied. "I be fine walkin'."

They shook hands and exchanged goodbyes. As his shoes hit the muck and the rain poured down on him, he let out a sigh of relief. Talking to Powell at times was like trying to empty a boiling pot: it needed to simmer down a bit before the deed was done. Yet the more and more he thought on it, the more and more his mind raced.

What *would* become of the Negro if slavery was abolished? What would be their lot in life, and how would that affect the world he knew?

As far as the old farmer was concerned, they did not deserve equal treatment under the law. Much like the Indian, so too was the Negro a species whose mind was limited and fragile. Even if such an effort was made to refine them, they did not have the know-how to handle more complex tasks. They most certainly could not run a business of their own...

But then again...

Did that necessarily mean that they deserved to be bound to a life of servitude? Did mothers deserve to be separated from their own children?

McLeary shook his head. *Quit stirrin' yerself up*, he thought. *Ye be turnin' a blind eye to the world yer whole life. No sense in carin' now.*

What was needed most was a cigar. A good cigar and a new set of clothes. And some alone time.

That was enough excitement for one day...

Chapter 6

Philadelphia, Pennsylvania
July 3, 1860

Streicher's mind raced. There were never enough hours in a day to get his tangled web of thoughts together. An ever-growing list overwhelmed him, and with the passing of each day he found it harder and harder to concentrate upon his work. There were a number of matters that needed to be attended to: He needed to find a home for himself and Emma; he needed to find the opportune moment to elope with her; he needed to find a place for them to be wed; he needed to find time to write an overdue letter of resignation (the very thought of it made him grin); he needed to find a way to give his father one final farewell (which, in all likelihood, would involve waving a certain finger); he needed to find...

He reclined in his chair and rubbed his eyes.

Or perhaps all his plans, in spite of their promise, were in vain. What seemed all the more likely was that he would eventually go mad and be condemned to a life of brick walls and stale bread.

He chuckled to himself.

That would not be such a bad alternative, all things considered. No punishment could match what he endured at the moment. Doyle's booming voice shook the walls of his office, and as the red-faced Irishman flailed his arms about, there was nothing more he could do than offer a nod every now and then. The bomb had been lit and there was no stopping it. Any attempt to do so was utterly useless.

"These southern states are a bit like children, you see," Doyle lectured to him. "Every so often, you have to give them a little spoonful of what they want to keep them quiet. But when they act up…" He plowed a fist into the palm of his hand. "Wham!" he yelled. "You come down on them, and you come down on them hard. Here lies the issue, lad: for too long these states have not been held accountable. They do what they want, and when the federal government tries to intervene, they denounce it as tyranny. Wrong!

What this country needs is a stronger central power. No longer can Washington be complicit to southern demands. *Someone* needs to bring the hand of justice to them, and if that means by force, so be it. We have a special candidate here, lad. Lincoln is the man who can put these states in their places. *He* will not tolerate oppositional voices, who have created a one-sided, corrupt system. *He* will do what is necessary to assert federal authority and not back down to southern interests. *He* will tell those slow-talking 'gentlemen' that their days of piggy-backing off Negroes are over, and that the West is free territory for *all* men. Mark my words, lad, and mark them well. *When* Lincoln wins, you will see the southern states plunge into turmoil. Their legislatures will run about like chickens without their heads, and when troops are sent their way, they will yield to federal supremacy."

At that, he let out a hearty laugh.

"To be honest with you," he continued, "there are times when I've thought about joining the ranks myself. I'd like to take a shot at one of those loud-mouthed, good-for-nothing sacks of rubbish and watch them run."

Streicher nodded slowly, his mind adrift and ever-thinking. It was not long before Doyle's rambunctious tirade grew numb to his ears. In time, he would begin a new life and all the pointless banter and posturing that came with his job would be buried in the past.

"Do those ears of yours work, Streicher?" Doyle questioned. "Come now, give me an answer."

"Hmm?"

The young man snapped out of his trance, and he met a frowning Doyle who stared at him expectantly with arms folded.

"I asked you a question," the Irishman stated, his tone firm and serious. "Would you take up arms for the cause?"

"Oh, uh…" he stammered. What exactly the 'cause' was left him guessing. Not that he cared much to look into it though. He knew what the right answer was. "Of course, sir. Without question."

Doyle eyed him carefully. "I don't know," he muttered. "To be frank with you, Streicher, I often wonder what you've got brewing in that head of yours. You have these flashes of such great potential — the makings of a true abolitionist. Then there are days such as these, when you're here in body and nothing more. Is something troubling you?"

"Sorry, sir." The young man offered a weak smile. "There's been a lot on my mind these past few weeks, is all. Personal things…"

Suddenly, the ends of Doyle's lips rose slightly. "Ah, I see…" he began slowly. "'Personal things,' eh? I've gone down that road myself more times than I care to admit. Dare I ask if there's a young lady involved in all of this?"

That's all I need, thought Streicher.

"There is," he mumbled.

"Aha!" came the shout. The Irishman rested a shoulder against the wall, and he gazed down upon the young man. "There always is, isn't there? What's the name of the lass who has sent the young Streicher's heart aflutter?"

Talk of southern states, abolition, and every controversy that came with such matters did not seem so intolerable now. Streicher reminded himself to mind his manners before replying, "Emma."

"Last name?"

Streicher paused.

"Come now, lad, out with it…"

"Hill."

"Emma Hill?"

"That's right, sir."

"She doesn't have the misfortune of being the daughter of that miser who owns Every Man Textiles, does she?" Doyle flashed a mischievous grin. When his remark was met with silence, his joking nature subsided and his cheeks were drained of their color. "You're not serious, are you?"

Streicher nodded.

Perhaps the occasion needed to be commemorated, Streicher mused to himself. At last, the great Shane Doyle was at a loss for words…

"Oh, well, I see…" Doyle struggled to string together a sentence. "Well, I'll say this for the man, his judgment of character must not be lost on him entirely if he approves of you."

"That's a bit of an assumption, if I may say so, sir," Streicher said, careful to not let a smirk cross his lips.

"What do you mean by that?"

"Let's say that I have grand intentions, which may or may not garner Mr. Hill's approval."

"Grand *intentions*?" Doyle raised an eyebrow. "And what exactly do you have your sights set on?"

"A future."

The Irishman let out an excited, almost childish yell. With a sweaty palm, he reached for the young man's hand and shook it firmly. Streicher, slightly startled but never fully surprised, had no choice but to accept it. He mustered a smile of his own.

"There he is!" Doyle proclaimed loudly for the whole city to hear. "Erich Streicher — a man of his own destiny! There's that rebellious spirit back at it, unrelenting and ever-present!"

"Thank you, sir."

"No reason the old hoot should ever know anything of the wedding," Doyle carried on. "None at all. Go exchange your vows, buy yourselves a home, and when that's all finished, tell that worthless pile of rubbish that he's got a better chance of drowning in his own saliva than he does of you surrendering his daughter over to him."

"Glad to," Streicher played along.

"And when your blessed day approaches," his voice shook with excitement, "I can expect an invitation to be sent my way?"

"You'll be first on the list, sir," Streicher matched his enthusiasm. There was something oddly satisfying about baiting his boss with a two-faced lie. It would be an appropriate send-off for a man who spent his days running his mouth and spewing lies about this or that. Yes, he would get Doyle's blood pumping. He would tell him, "Any day now, sir, you'll get what's yours…" Then, on the fateful day that seemed all the more real with the chime of every hour, Doyle would find a letter from him that contained a special notice, complete with 'Regrettably, I must part ways from the company…'

and 'Here's to a brighter tomorrow for us both.' Signed — Yours truly, Good ol' Dixie.

The young man could not help but let out a laugh. Doyle was too caught up in his own excitement to notice.

"This is cause for celebration, my boy!" the Irishman exclaimed. "Tonight, you and I are going to get ourselves a few drinks."

"But sir…"

"That's not a request," he interrupted. "If any of your folks have questions, tell them you've got to work a late night before the holiday."

Streicher mulled it over. Free drinks in exchange for an evening with his boss. He could think of other ways to enjoy a night, but at least they were closed on the Fourth of July. With any luck, he would get lost in his drinks and become oblivious of that blabbering hothead.

"I can count on you then, lad, can't I?"

Streicher smiled. "Wherever you want me to meet you, I'll be there, sir."

Doyle gave him a slap on the back. "Good man!" he said. "Give me some time to weigh our options, and then we'll have ourselves a night!"

***

Streicher wound his way through crowded streets and dark alleys. A pale crescent moon glistened in a starless sky. It never ceased to amaze him how the city never slept, even on the eve of a holiday. Then again, it was bound to erupt even more so than usual in a mere twenty-four hours, given the occasion. The sky would be lit up in shades of red, white, and blue, and he would gaze upon the spectacle in silent fascination.

It would not be such a chore to indulge in a beer or two to kick off the holiday, and he would have time to contemplate his future. Streicher bit his lip. The latter, although abundant with hope, made his stomach churn uneasily for several reasons. For one, guilt weighed upon him more and more as each day passed. He had not spoken to Emma since the night they were parted, and thoughts of her lying awake with teary eyes and a broken heart sent him tossing and turning each night. He had not so much as sent her a letter, which was due in large part to him not having the faintest idea how she would receive it. Visions of her father toyed with his mind. Bearing the brunt of his rage had been an experience that he did not wish to repeat. But he had to contact her soon, if nothing more than to let her know that he had not given up on their future.

Second, it seemed like he knew very little about how to make their dreams a reality. In the days that crept by since the party, he had glanced at a newspaper here and there, watchful for any job opportunities. Headlines promised fresh starts in the West, but that came with the immense responsibility of being largely self-sufficient. As a city boy, he knew he would not be able to provide for them in that kind of environment. Of course, the prospect of simply grabbing a suitcase and taking the first train southbound was an alternative… but was it a wise decision? They would not know anyone; they would not know where they were. If national tensions truly threatened to boil over, would it be in their best interests to relocate anywhere below the Mason-Dixon line? And what if inquiring minds were curious of his employment history? He was not by any means a betting man, but he wagered that his abolitionist works would not be well-received.

Third, and perhaps most peculiar of all, that same guilt crept upon him as he pondered his resignation. In a matter of hours, when the dreams of the future subsided and he was forced back to reality, the idea of burning bridges gave him pause. It was not leaving the job itself that messed with his conscience — he never cared much for it to begin with — but the thought of springing an unexpected surprise on his boss seemed unnecessary. Doyle was not a bad man; he had never shown him any disrespect or indifference. In fact, he had often looked upon him as a valued asset to his business, and in that way, Streicher could not speak badly of him. Sure, Doyle had strong opinions, but his passion was also strangely admirable, and the fact that he was never afraid to make his views known to anyone gave Streicher a sense of comfort. If anyone sought to stir up trouble with Streicher, he knew (gratefully so) that they would first have to answer to his boss.

His thoughts left him shaking his head. *Get ahold of yourself,* he demanded. *Face it — the only reason you're giving Doyle the benefit of the doubt now is because he's treating you tonight. You wouldn't have blinked an eye about leaving him if he hadn't thrown together this little outing.*

He arrived at the entrance to the Broken Mug, which looked pretty much as he expected it would: a decrepit, two-story wooden building that ran rampant with large cracks and jagged splinters. A cutout of a dark, faded pint dangled beneath the sign, and although it had been purposefully withered and broken down, it seemed as if nature's elements had given it an even greater beating. Wide, glaring eyes fixed upon him as he entered a sprawling room, dark and musty, that held congregations of card-players and seedy characters. Many of the customers were large, burly men who had just finished a long day of hard labor. As they cast a glance at his faded clothes and tattered shoes (the attire was intentional), all parties resumed their private business, no longer paying him any mind.

The bar was fixed along the wall on the right side, and aside from a few scattered pairs, the counter was mostly vacant. Doyle was seated at the far end, and once he spotted the young man, he gave him a wave and hollered for him to come over. Streicher took a seat beside him, and the bartender met his gaze and raised an eyebrow. "Drink?"

"Oh, uh…" Streicher stammered, " give me a beer, please. Something light that I won't regret later…"

Doyle laughed. "Not much of a drinker, eh?" he asked. "Come now, where's that German blood in you?"

"Don't want to overdo it today," Streicher answered politely.

As the bartender returned with a bubbling pint, Doyle muttered to him, "Put it on my tab."

"Thank you, sir."

"Pleasure's mine, lad." Doyle took a swig from his own drink. "Now, let's talk a bit more about this future of yours, shall we?"

"Sure," Streicher answered, trying in vain to match his enthusiasm.

"To your credit," the Irishman began, "you'll be sticking it to a man who, if I'm being truthful, is not to be trifled with. Robert Hill is a man of power, a city elite, and as such he has many connections. That said, Streicher, you have the heart of a lion, much like me. You're not afraid to kick up some muck, and you're not afraid to tell men like Hill to get off their high horse."

Streicher's throat became dry. If his boss was trying to assure him of his decision, he was not doing a very good job of it. If his plan did come to fruition, Hill would be after him. "Speaking of Mr Hill," he said, trying to divert the conversation slightly, "if you don't mind me asking, what sort of quarrel do you have with him? Is it a personal matter?"

"Personal?" Doyle repeated, slightly surprised. "There's nothing personal about it. In fact, I couldn't tell you hardly anything about the man himself. What I do know is that he earns his money off the backs of slaves, and that's enough for me to blast him to kingdom come."

"And you're not concerned with any sort of…" Streicher paused, trying to think of the right word, "*retribution*?"

"From Hill?" Doyle let out a howl of laughter. "Good heavens, Streicher, there's your comedic genius back at it again. Lad, I have blasted the scum of this city's 'elite' for years, and I can assure you that Robert Hill is no different from the rest. You need to understand something: these slavers and those that do business with them are born of a different breed. Money is their only love and as long as they keep raking it in, they're content. Sure, I get under Hill's skin every now and then — I get under the skin of a lot of people — but as long as I keep away from his share of the pot, he won't so much as turn in my direction." Doyle grinned mischievously and rubbed his hands together. "Of course," he added, "don't think I haven't considered the idea once or twice."

Streicher sipped his beer and sat in silence. For some reason, the Shane Doyle who sat beside him seemed different than the one who ran his mouth at work. In the office, he denounced society's injustices and fumed about the evils of slavery. Yet here he sat , treating his business as if it was only sport. A game in which he was an active participant. Perhaps the real reason he kicked mud on the rest of the world had nothing to do with righting wrongs or fighting inequalities. Perhaps it had *only* to do with the satisfaction that came from getting a rise out of others. In and of itself, it was a dangerous game to play, but if there was ever a man who was worthy enough to compete, it was Doyle. The realization struck Streicher like a violent wave, and his thoughts were scattered.

They spent the next hour discussing a wide array of topics — how Streicher and Emma came to know each other, how life at the Streicher household had been (his father was largely glossed over), and the trials and tribulations of Doyle and his wife (as he joked, it was a 'losing battle' as soon as he put the ring on her finger). The conversation was tame enough, and as Streicher glanced at his empty pint, his will to leave grew stronger. He hoped Doyle would take the hint, but after ordering another round, it appeared that their friendly outing would become an all-night affair.

The Irishman held his glass high and smiled. "Happy Fourth, lad!" he declared. "When the clock strikes midnight, may the righteous prosper and the wicked crumble!"

Another bellowing laugh rang out as the two men clinked their glasses. As his laughing spell began to subside, Doyle focused his gaze towards the entrance to the pub. His jovial demeanor faded slightly and a look of concern took its place. "There's a sore sight." Doyle gestured towards the entrance. "A girl like that shouldn't be in a place like this."

Streicher turned his head and nearly fell to the floor at who he saw. There she stood, sporting a silky maroon dress. Her pale skin glistened softly in the dim light. The entire room grew silent, captivated by her simple beauty. Streicher nearly stumbled off his stool as he raced towards her. "Emma!"

Her crystal blue eyes grew wide at the sight of him, and the two embraced tightly. Joy and surprise overcame Streicher: a reunion was entirely unexpected, especially in such a sleazy place.

Questions scurried through his mind, and as he struggled to find the right ones to ask, his mouth spilled everything for him. "What are you doing here?" he asked. "How did you know where I'd be? What if your father…"

She held a finger to his lips and smiled. "You're babbling again," she teased.

Streicher felt his cheeks grow warm and a crooked smile came to his lips. "But…" he stammered, "I don't understand…"

"My father's out celebrating the holiday with some of his friends," Emma said. "I figured it'd be the perfect opportunity to see what you were up to."

"You went to my house?"

She nodded. "Your mother told me about your little night on the town," she continued. "She said I shouldn't come here alone, but what can I say? It's been too long…"

"You *shouldn't* have." Streicher spoke softly. "This isn't the kind of place you should be at. If your father finds out…"

"He won't."

"How do you know?"

"He likes to stay out late on holidays."

"What time do you think he'll be back?"

"Not sure," Emma shrugged. "After midnight, that much I can tell you."

"I… that's wonderful," was all he could manage to say. "We've got a few hours then. Does anyone else know you're gone?"

"I told one of the maids," she answered, "that I was going to be out visiting a friend."

"And she bought it?"

"You bet." Emma's smile grew wider. "Even told me to have a great time."

"Incredible." Streicher shook his head in awe. "What can I say, Emma? You never cease to amaze me."

"What about your boss?" she asked. "Is he still here?"

Streicher froze. The possibility, rather, *inevitability* of his loud-mouthed, drunken boss making an appearance put a damper on a night that held (albeit briefly) tremendous potential. Before he could answer, the booming voice called out from behind him.

"Well, well…" Doyle cooed as he strolled over with a pint in his hand. He flashed Emma a beaming smile. "So, this is Emma, eh? The lad speaks of you quite fondly, miss. I think you've stole his heart."

Streicher blushed. "Emma," he said quietly, "please meet my boss, Mr. Shane Doyle."

The two of them bowed their heads politely and exchanged pleasantries. Doyle turned to Streicher and gave him a friendly pat on the shoulder. "If you wanted to bring your lass along," he said, "all you had to do was ask."

Streicher opened his mouth to speak, but Emma beat him to it. "This was a bit of a surprise, sir," she stated. "Erich didn't know I was coming."

"So you did in fact come here by yourself?"

"Yes, sir."

"You're brave, dear," he commented. "This isn't the kind of place where young women should be wandering around alone."

"I suppose not," she replied, not caring much to dwell on the subject any longer.

"Well, in any case, you're here safe and sound. And Streicher can take you back home when you've had enough, right, lad?"

"Yes, sir."

"You two enjoy yourselves." Doyle smiled. "I'll be over by the bar, getting in the 'proper' mood for the holiday. Get yourselves whatever you want — it's on me."

They thanked him for his generosity, and as they meandered their way towards a small table in the far corner of the room, Doyle called over, "Oh, and one more thing, Miss Hill…"

"Yes, sir?"

"Send your father my regards, will you?" He winked at Streicher and flashed that wicked grin yet again.

Once they sat down at the table, Emma ordered a glass of wine and Streicher went against his better judgement by ordering another beer.

"Interesting," Emma remarked. "My father and your boss do business together?"

Streicher laughed uneasily. "It's more like my boss makes your father's hair turn grey."

"Ah, I see…"

"Listen, Emma," Streicher began, "I'm sorry for not reaching out to you. I didn't know how…"

"Don't be," she said dismissively, shaking her head. "It's better you didn't write to me. My father's been uptight ever since the party, and I think he's on the lookout for anything with your name on it. It's better this way, to meet in person."

"Of course," he agreed. "In that case, what do you think? Are you still okay with our plan?"

"I am," she answered, albeit reluctantly.

"Emma, if you're serious about this, you need to be entirely on board. What's the matter?"

"Look, Erich," she began slowly, careful of her words, "I *am* serious. I want a future with you, but we need to think about all we're leaving behind."

"Like what?"

"Well, consider your family, for instance."

"I'll write to my mother. My father can brew about it all day, every day, for all I care."

"What about your job?"

"I'll find another one," he answered, slightly surprised by his quick response.

"You're sure?"

"Certain."

"And Mr. Doyle, you're sure you won't miss…"

"It's all a game to him," Streicher said, careful to keep his voice low. "He just wants to get in people's faces and tell them he's right. Believe me, I can find someone else to work for."

"Okay," Emma said uneasily. "If you say so…"

"Be honest with me," he urged. "If there's a problem, I need to know about it. Are you having doubts?"

"I wouldn't say doubts," she answered. "Make no mistake, I want to marry you, Erich. I want the future to be *our* future, but what was said at the party… we didn't think it through. All I'm saying is that we should take some more time to weigh our options and consider if leaving everything behind is really what we want to do. I mean, that's quite a sacrifice to turn our backs on everything we know, regardless of whether we like it or not."

"Seeing how both of our fathers stand in all of this," Streicher countered, "I don't know if we have much of a choice. Let's look at the facts for what they are: if my father has it his way, I'm marrying a Protestant girl. If your father has it his way, you'll be stuck with some pompous fool."

"I guess you're right," she concluded, sighing.

"Emma?"

"Hmmm?"

"You're sure you want to marry me?"

"Of course," she answered. Her eyes, honest and pure, twinkled in the pale light.

"Good then," he stated, and his smile returned. "We've got to look out for each other, okay? And there's still so much to look forward to…"

Emma nodded her head excitedly, trying hard to hold back joyful tears.

"Then how about this…" Streicher offered. "Why don't we wait until after the election to move somewhere? Say, perhaps, the middle or end of November? That'll give us some time to make our plans, and we'll figure out where we want to live. I'll even have time to put in a resignation notice for work. What do you think?"

Emma happily agreed, and when the drinks were brought to the table, they clinked their glasses in celebration. It was a distant dream, but before long it would become a reality. As far as Streicher was concerned, that was all that mattered.

**

The evening was filled with laughter and seemingly endless conversation. They discussed Emma's fascination with books, particularly romantic literature. She rattled off names and titles, but all Streicher could do was nod every now and then and put forth a friendly smile. He had always known her to be an intellectual, and it was her keen desire to acquire more refined tastes that he found quite appealing. At the same time, she never held herself in higher regard compared to the rest of society, which was a special quality that very few of her peers possessed. She was adaptable to any situation, any audience..

The topic shifted slightly as she declared her own interest in writing a book, an 'epic,' as she called it. As she delved into her fantasy world, describing her heroine — a queen who longed to break free from her obligations and run off with a condemned prisoner — she briefly paused and cast a puckered grin towards Streicher. "Am I boring you?" she teased.

"Not at all," Streicher responded, slightly dazed. "Continue, please…"

"We can come back to it later," she said, laughing. "What about you?"

"What about me?"

"Have you read any good books lately?"

"You know me, Emma," he remarked, smiling. "I'm a writer, not a reader."

"I thought you couldn't be one without being the other," she winked.

"Like anything else, there's exceptions to the rule."

"I guess so," she chuckled and took a sip of her wine. "Well, considering what you do for a living, let me ask you this... Have you ever read *Uncle Tom's Cabin*?"

Now it was Streicher's turn to laugh. "I've taken a glance at it," he confessed, "but nothing more. Doyle was trying to get me to read it a few weeks ago — apparently it's a master work."

"It is."

"You've read it?"

Emma nodded. "Without my father knowing, of course," she added. "You know how he feels about the abolitionist cause..."

"No need to tell me twice," he nodded. "Can't say that I blame him for it either, if I'm being truthful."

"I beg your pardon?" Emma chuckled, but it was forced. "Might I remind you of who you work for?"

"I know exactly who I work for, but that doesn't mean I agree with him."

"Why do you work for him then?"

"Because he gives me a living wage," he said. "I'd just as much write for some pro-slavery half-wit, so long as the money is good."

"Let me get this straight then," Emma prodded further, "you don't believe the slaves should be emancipated?"

"Never thought much about it." Streicher shrugged. "I take it you do?"

"Of course," her voice rose slightly. "It's an inhumane practice, and quite frankly, the very root of this country's trouble."

"Maybe it is; maybe it isn't."

"I…" The words fled her.

"Are you okay, Emma?" Streicher asked. "My apologies, I didn't mean to offend you."

"Oh, no, you're…" she fumbled for her words. "No offense taken."

Silence.

"Everything alright, Emma?"

"Fine."

"Please, tell me…"

"You really don't have a thought one way or the other about it?"

"About what? Slavery?"

She nodded.

The young man shifted in his chair. "Quite truthfully," he began, "I do believe that there is a place for the Negro in American society. That being said, I don't think too fondly on the prospect of the Negro being 'equal,' per se. His work is to be of a humble means, nothing more. Out in the fields, that's where he should be… not among white folks, and certainly not in high society.

What the abolitionists are proposing is dangerous. What will happen to the supply line if slaves are freed? That house of yours, grand as it is, could no longer be in your father's possession if southern planters are ruined. Then, you must keep in mind the more… *far-reaching* implications of their freedom. If slaves are freed, then surely they'd have to garner greater representation. In that case, there may even be an argument to grant Negro men *suffrage*. That is another dangerous prospect, for no other reason than a good share of the voting population would be uneducated, illiterate. How can we ensure that that shift among voters would not endanger our political stability?"

"Only time will tell, I suppose," Emma muttered. "It's all too much at times…"

"That's why we need to turn our backs on it all," he reminded her. "Emma, these political 'dilemmas,' or whatever you choose to call them, are insignificant. They are for politicians to figure out. What *I* want, more than anything, is for you and I to get away from the rest of the world. I want a life of peace and happiness for the two of us, that's all. We'll raise some children along the way, make good memories as a family. It's all an honest man could *ever* want."

She smiled at him, and the pair conjured visions of a new life, one in which they could chart their own course. Their thoughts were often naïve and whimsical,

Streicher could not deny. Certainly, there would be bumps in the road along the way, but no marriage was perfect. As he finished off his pint and sat content in a hazy stupor, he cast a glance across the room. Doyle was flailing his arms about, his face red and lively, and attempted to lure the bartender and surrounding patrons to hear his sermon about one injustice or another. His performance, animated as it was, was met with eyerolls and shaking heads.

Good luck, folks, he thought, chuckling. He returned his attention to Emma, who had turned around in her chair and was fixated upon something near the entrance. "Something wrong?" he asked. His question was met with trembling eyes and a pale complexion. It looked as if she was about to grow faint. Immediately, Streicher collected his wits and reached for her hand. "Emma…"

"It's my father," she whispered, her voice grave and weak. "He's spotted us…"

Before he could respond, the tall, thin frame of Robert Hill came into view. His hair was ruffled slightly, and he was dressed in a black suit that appeared a bit too untidy, sloppy. His tie hung lazily around the collar and the jacket had traces of dark splotches, probably dustings of dirt or debris. But that mattered little to Streicher, who looked into the eyes of a man whose rage sank into a new darkness. As he barreled his way towards the table, the young man could do nothing more than raise his hands in protest.

"'Out with a friend,' is that it?" Hill's words were as sharp as talons. "Young lady, I will make sure you rue this day."

"Father…" Emma choked out, as if it was a desperate plea. "Please keep Erich out of this."

"Oh, don't worry," he snapped, not bothering to cast a glance in his direction, "after speaking to *his* father, I'd say he's got problems of his own."

He grabbed his daughter by the wrist and hoisted her to her feet. Almost instinctively, Streicher rose from his seat. "We're getting out of this place," Hill fumed. "Our carriage is waiting out front, and I don't want to hear a word from you on the way home. Do you understand me?"

She nodded timidly and gave Streicher one last pitiful look.

"Sir, please wait," Streicher called out. "We can talk this over…"

Hill spun around to meet him, eyes wide and veins popping. One hand was still clamped to his daughter's wrist; the other was clenched into a fist. Streicher held up his hands defensively and took a step away from him. "Say another word, boy," Hill challenged, those dark beads tearing into him, "and I will knock you into next week."

A shrill laugh rang out. Doyle strolled towards them, hunched over slightly, with tears rolling down his cheeks. Apparently, he had concluded his tirade and set his sights on another, far more intriguing pursuit. He folded his arms across his chest and greeted Hill with a crooked grin. "You're a kidder, Hill," the Irishman taunted. "I'd like to see those fists of fury at work."

"Keep that thick tongue of yours clicking," the other warned, "and you just might."

Doyle's smile grew wider. "Really?" he challenged. "I'll bet those hands of yours are good for ass-grabbing, but that's about it."

Hill paused, frozen in a state of untapped anger, and then he rushed towards him. The two men stood mere inches apart, with Hill towering above him. Streicher stood paralyzed, uncertain whether intervening would make the situation worse. Emma locked eyes with him in mute panic, begging him to do something.

"Listen to me, you conniving weasel," Hill's voice shook. "Do. Not. Test. Me."

"Why not?" the Irishman baited him, his smile still fixed to his lips.

"Because I'm half-tempted to reach down and throttle that neck of yours," he threatened. "You'd better watch yourself, Doyle. A man as short as you shouldn't be letting his mouth run amuck."

"I wouldn't be so sure of that," Doyle fired back. "A man as short as I could reach out and grab those crown jewels of yours and rip them from your trousers."

He paused, allowing his teeth to glow in the dim light, and added, "Then again, maybe that's giving you too much credit. After all, a cent-sucking leech such as yourself is no man."

Pale-faced and clammy, Streicher watched as the taller man slammed a hard fist into his foe's abdomen. Doyle staggered backwards, clutching at his stomach and gasping for air. Refusing to break stride, Hill marched over to him, grasped him firmly by the collar, and delivered another sharp jab that collided against the side of his jaw. The Irishman let out a gasp and tumbled to the wooden floor.

Apparently satisfied with his quick work, Hill backed away from him slightly. "Hear this, and hear it well." His icy tone pierced the air. "Your days of slandering my name are over."

Streicher glanced around to find dozens of eyes trained upon them, eager to see what more would come of the scuffle. Several men stood to the side with arms folded, ready to step in and separate them (or participate, Streicher could not be sure). Just as he found the nerve to speak up, a wide-eyed Doyle, with that slap-happy grin still intact, came to his feet and lumbered towards Hill. With his back turned, Hill's eyes bulged as burly arms clamped around him and tackled him to the ground. An emphatic cheer rang out from the crowd as Doyle took the upper hand and began delivering a volley of heavy-handed blows.

A hard knock to Hill's nose spurred Streicher to action. Once he came forward to separate them, so too did a few other men. By the end of it, a sweat-soaked Doyle reveled in the excitement of the crowd, declaring his victory to be 'justice served, sweet and sound.' Hill

113

was helped to his feet, and he had to take a few moments to free himself from a dreary haze. It was not long before the carriage driver rushed in, and at the sight of him, he hurried over and gave him a handkerchief to quell his bloody nose. As the two of them limped out of the pub, Streicher and Emma kissed quickly and promised that they would see each other again in the coming week.

Doyle was dubbed the 'workman's hero' by the regulars of the Broken Mug. It was a decisive victory by the working-class commoner against a shining example of the city's snobbish elite. Although the celebration was jovial, with spirited cheers and drinks flowing, it had been put to an early end. Wanting no more trouble, the owner asked for Doyle and his 'pal' to make their way out. Such a request was met with strong disapproval from the crowd, and Doyle did his best to make a show of it. Before long, Streicher escorted his boss out of the tavern. Still racing with excitement, the Irishman sang tunes and uttered joyful cries, declaring Streicher to be 'a million-dollar man.'

At an intersection, the two men parted ways. Fatigued and numb, Streicher sauntered towards his home. With any luck, his father would chew him out in the morning. More than anything, he wanted to rest his head on a soft pillow and drift away to a dreamless sleep.

That was enough excitement for one day…

Chapter 7

Powell Plantation, Virginia
July 4, 1860

It was a cold chill that came upon him. As the carriage lumbered its way down the cobblestone path to the palace, there was something about the freshly-cut lawn and white pillars that made McLeary uneasy. The last time he set foot on the property, he had returned a wounded young slave to her owner. Well-intentioned though his actions may have been, the old farmer could not help but let that day fester in his memory like a disease.

"Don't get yourself in a fit," Alice had advised him. "You've done a good service, Thomas. The poor girl would've ended up worse off if you let her go."

It was that possibility, and that possibility alone, that provided McLeary with a slight sense of comfort. Albeit a reluctant one, his decision had been made and the choice had been clear: Betty needed to be returned to her master. After all, what would have happened if he had allowed her to push forward in her quest? Nothing good would have come of it, that much was certain. She would have been captured, and as the gavel was about to come down upon her, she might very well have informed the authorities of a certain farmer who had been compassionate enough to see her on her way. And whatever consequences would have come about from *that*, McLeary did not wish to think on it.

He sat dressed in a black suit (a habit which was becoming a bit too frequent lately for his liking), and in his lap rested a large tin box. Alice sat beside him in a pale blue dress. A string of pearls sat comfortably around her neck, and she gazed silently out the window. The evening's preparations were long and unnecessary, McLeary believed. His wife had become so preoccupied with applying the finishing touches to her appearance that she had forgotten about the time. Much to McLeary's frustration, they had strolled out the door late, and they would be among the last of the stragglers to arrive at the party.

"This be the reason why them parties ain't worth the treble," McLeary had said, lecturing her. "Alice, we's gonna be lyin' in our graves if you ain't makin' haste."

After a bit of back-and-forth, they found their way to the carriage. All that mattered now was that they had made it to the plantation, and Powell would be very pleased to see the little treasure chest that he brought along with him.

"Now you's gonna see dis place jumpin'," the driver called back to them with a laugh. "Misstuh Powell be real glad you's gonna be here tonight."

They were greeted at the entrance by Sampson, who offered a friendly smile and held the door open for them. As they entered, their nostrils were flooded with thick smoke. A light haze clouded the grand entrance as men waved around cigars in one hand and drinks in the other. It was a wild, rambunctious outing as choruses of laughter, hollers, and spirited cheers rang out in the decadent hall. A handful of slaves hurried about the room feverishly, refilling glasses and wiping down counters. Alice huddled close to her husband as they followed Sampson down the hall. In the midst of the frenzy, the whirlwind of conversations grew clearer, and every now and then a voice was heard.

"Lincoln will be the downfall of this great country; God forbid he's elected!"

"We ourselves are slaves to federal authority, that's what the truth is!"

"John Brown got what he deserved, and let any traitor take his place if such an insurrection should happen again!"

In the back parlor, the smoke grew thicker and the ruckus, even louder. Powell stood at the head of a large, circular table, holding court, with a cigar wedged in between his lips. A grin was stuck to his face. He shuffled a deck of cards, letting them slip through his fingers, and he then fired them to four men seated around him. "Alright, gentlemen," he declared, "I want a clean game this time, you hear? A *clean* game…"

His eyes shifted momentarily, and as he cast his gaze upon his two guests, a spark lit up his pupils. His grin grew wider, and he gestured flamboyantly in their direction. "Ah, yes, here they come!" he announced. Alice flashed a wide smile as heads turned to face them. McLeary cracked a half-hearted smirk.

"So, this is the famous Thomas McLeary?" a scruffy, older gentleman asked. He was trim, slender, and sported a charcoal grey hat, which matched his jacket.

"In the flesh," Powell nodded. "And his lovely wife…"

The man bowed his head politely towards Alice. "How do you do, ma'am?"

Alice curtseyed, eyes radiant with charm, and returned the nod. "It's a pleasure," she said.

"Indeed, it is," Powell remarked and put forth a stream of smoke from his lips. "I do apologize for the… 'frivolities,' shall we say? Rest assured, Mrs. McL… *Alice*…" — he gave her a wink — "…that the ladies are in the living room. I doubt you'd care much to spend time in a circus such as this."

His statement was met with a chuckle. "Please, Henry," she said, blushing, "all that matters is that you and your pals are having a good time."

"I'd say we are, isn't that right, gentlemen?" Three of the four men nodded. The loner, a young man who sat slumped to the left of Powell, remained stone-faced. He was a large, burly fellow whose trunks for arms lay crossed. "Sampson," Powell called to his slave. "Do me a favor and show Alice to the other room, please. We shall all reconvene for a late dinner."

McLeary found another reason why trips to Powell's place were becoming increasingly difficult. The planter's charm was running a bit too strong for his liking, especially when it was directed towards his wife. In the time McLeary had known her, Alice always had a certain charm as well, having hailed from Richmond's high society. But it seemed that what was shared between her and the planter was an overt affection, playful though it may have been, that tested McLeary's patience. She was better off in the other room, and when it came time for dinner, she would sit as far away from that man as possible.

The farmer laid the tin box at the center of the table, and immediately reaching hands went about claiming their treasures. McLeary sat himself beside a portly, middle-aged gentlemen, whose balding hairline suggested that he might have been older than he looked. He looked at the fourth member of the group, who sat to the right of Powell. An older man with small glasses and curly salt-and-pepper hair studied his deck intently as he puffed away on one of McLeary's beauties.

"Y'all had best enjoy this special treat." Powell smiled. "McLeary's cigars are the best in the country, and you can bet your lives on it that this supply won't be leaving our table."

A string of laughter echoed in the small room.

"My, oh my," the balding man twirled his piping stick and gave him a friendly smile. "Sir, this is remarkable…"

"Thanks," McLeary muttered, not bothering to match his enthusiasm.

"McLeary," Powell called to him, "how about joining us in our game? We're about to start…" The planter paused and let out a hearty laugh. He shook his head and thumped a hand against his temple. "Lord have mercy." He chuckled. "My age seems to be catching up to me. A bit too quickly for my liking. McLeary, allow me the pleasure of introducing this fine cohort…"

He gestured to the man with the glasses. "This here," he said, "is Dr Herman Knouse. He served with me out west during the war."

Knouse looked up from his cards and nodded politely.

Next, it was the man with the grey hat…

"George Brennan," Powell continued. "He's an old pal of mine — we've done business together over the years."

Brennan tipped his cap and offered a friendly, "It's a pleasure, sir."

"Beside you is Edward Collett," he went on. "I met him at an auction down in Atlanta a while back, and the rest as they say is history."

Collett extended a hand and the two men shook. Just as Powell gestured to the young man beside him, he appeared stiff and rigid, as if his gleeful façade was slowly deteriorating.

"This fellow here," Powell's tone was slightly tense, "goes by the name of Buck. He's the son of a dear friend of mine who passed away some years ago — bless his soul. Every now and then, I invite the boy up here to indulge in a nice vacation."

McLeary eyed the young man, who glared back at him with a blazing fire in his eyes. He sat frozen like a statue with his arms still folded. He had not bothered to even shift his gaze when McLeary's offerings were brought to the table. There was a hardness about him that caused the old farmer to shift in his seat. A raw silence tainted the air. For a reason unknown, he felt challenged by his presence, his sheer size. The boy had the makings of a bull, and instinct told him that it was best to keep on his good side.

"These pals of mine," Powell's voice fought to regain its cheerfulness, "hail from the great state of South Carolina. Charleston, to be specific. Well, all except for Buck. He was born and raised in the heart of farm country. Isn't that right, boy?"

Buck nodded his head slowly, eyes still locked upon McLeary. The farmer felt his lips turn dry. *Tonight ain't gonna end soon nuff*, he thought miserably.

The game was poker, and it lasted far too long for McLeary's liking. He tossed a chip into the pile every now and then, hoping desperately that someone would call his bluff and take him out of the game. The rules were far too complicated for him to take an interest in it, and given that he never cared much to play cards to begin with, the desire to learn was not strong.

It was a civil game up until the end. Buck's stone-cold demeanor sent him toe-to-toe against Knouse, who mustered up a commendable poker face of his own. Ultimately, age and experience prevailed, and the doctor held the winning hand. At the realization of his defeat, Buck slammed a fist so hard upon the table that it rocked their glasses and sent one shattering to the floor. By the time the mess was cleaned, a consensus came about: poker was finished for the night. Not that McLeary minded, of course. He would have preferred drowning in his guilt and misery to having to play another round. It was only when questioning eyes turned to meet him that he wished they would play again.

"I've been told you're a man who doesn't dwell too much upon political matters," Brennan said with a teasing smile. "It's not that I don't trust my source, but I find it hard to believe that *any* man is without an opinion these days."

"It's true." Collett wedged an elbow in his side. "Nowadays, it seems like everyone's trying to get in the final word."

McLeary held up a hand. "Don' take me for rude or nothin'," the farmer started, "but what're ye tryin' to say? Am I supposed to got 'n opinion on somethin'?"

"That's for you to decide, sir," Brennan said, laughing. "Let's take this election, for example. Who do you believe is the ideal candidate for the White House?"

"I dunno." McLeary shrugged. "Ain't concern me one way or 'nother."

"It better," Buck chimed in, his voice low and gruff, "if ye got any sense to look out for yerself."

"Whad'ya mean?"

"Lincoln," Brennan answered emphatically. "You're a bright man, McLeary, and if you've got any sense, you'll know who *not* to vote for, at the very least."

"In our state," Collett remarked, "we have it easy because that matter will already be resolved by the time we get to the polls."

"Huh?"

"Lincoln's not going to be on the ballot," Knouse informed him. "I reckon other states will adopt the same policy."

"Virginia better be the next to strike his name," Powell scoffed. "That's all we need is for *him* to pull the strings in Washington."

"Ain't that sorta thang fiddlin' with, er…"

"It ain't fiddlin'." Buck cut him off. "If it means savin' our way o' life, there ain't no wrongdoin'."

"Lincoln's a threat to the stability of our country," Brennan said, lecturing to him. "The agenda of the Republican Party is destructive. They wish to turn this country on its head."

"It's the truth," agreed Knouse. "The Republicans cry out for abolition, but what, I ask, is their solution if that is to come to fruition?"

"It ain't gonna," Buck muttered. "Not if I got somethin' to say 'bout it…"

"There's a lot of good land to be found between here and the Pacific," Collett stated, "and slave labor is what's needed to make the most of it. If the Republicans take control, the future of the West will be thrown into chaos."

"As if Bleeding Kansas wasn't enough…" Powell shook his head in disgust. "This country doesn't need something like that happening again. And it most certainly does *not* need another John Brown leading the way."

"Mark my words," Brennan said, "Lincoln *is* the next John Brown. In fact, he's more than that. He's *dangerous*, and a man as deranged as he is should not be able to entertain the *thought* of becoming president."

Everyone agreed, and eventually the conversation returned to casual banter and quick jokes. Time dragged on as each of the men (except Buck) dove into too much detail about their personal lives, sharing precious memories and tales that McLeary cared little about. At last, Sampson returned and whispered in Powell's ear.

The planter nodded excitedly, which prompted Collett to ask, "Dinner's ready, eh, Henry?"

"Only a little while longer," Powell replied. "I have a special guest that I'd like all of you to meet first."

Powell hurried out of the room with Sampson trailing closely behind. The men exchanged curious glances with one another, and when the planter returned, a young man strolled along beside him. He was everything a gentleman aspired to be — handsome, trim, and clean-cut. He had a dark moustache, and its color matched the color of the curls atop his head. Eyes widened across the table, awestruck by a man whose reputation was so profound that he could not be ignored. Even Buck, whose stone-faced persona was unrivaled, had a twinkle in his eye.

Once again, McLeary was lost. The stranger bore no meaning or significance to him, and the thought of meeting another acquaintance was enough to make his head pound. He reclined in his chair and took in a long draw from his cigar.

Brennan spoke up, his voice filled with wonder. "Is he who I think he is?"

Powell's smile beamed as he gestured to his guest. "Why, yes, he is, George," the planter exalted. "My good sirs, may I introduce to you the one and only — Mr. John Wilkes Booth!"

***

McLeary began to wonder whether Booth was a valued guest or the entertainment for the evening. All heads turned to face him at dinner, and he took great pleasure in receiving the attention. His flair and flamboyancy — the way he exaggerated his body language and adjusted his pitch — was a special combination that kept his audience entranced. One moment, his veins popped and his voice thundered, and then the next, his jaw slackened and his tone slipped down to a soothing whisper.

From what McLeary bothered to gather, he hailed from a family of actors, and his career sent him performing before audiences across the country, from Boston to New Orleans. The guests adored his quirky antics and theatrics, and the entire room shook with laughter whenever he poked fun at those living above the Mason-Dixon line.

McLeary spent nearly the entire time poking and prodding at the pork and collard greens on his plate. There was something about Booth that made his stomach churn, and he was unsure whether to be impressed by him or appalled. Behind that façade, which was so greatly animated and expressive, was a man who had a certain smugness about him. Maybe it was the way that he paused, when he let the corner of his lip rise ever so slightly, that revealed him to be someone consumed by his own vanity. He was cocky, arrogant, and what came with him was a sense of entitlement that only the most privileged were familiar with. What did he know of a hard day's work?

A face like that ain't gonna survive out 'n fields, McLeary thought, shaking his head. *Go on 'n' make a jackass o' yerself.*

Once the meal concluded, the party gradually filtered out of the room, with Booth leading much of the crowd to the grand hall. Alice conversed in earnest with several ladies at the table, and McLeary took advantage of the opportunity to take his brandy and slip out to the back porch. The sky was painted purple as the sun dipped beneath the horizon. A respectable breeze brushed the tranquil fields, and he watched in silence as slaves retired to their quarters for the night.

His eyes narrowed as a sharp, rhythmic ring echoed in the distance. With a shaking hand, he raised his glass to his lips and took a long sip. There was her silhouette, etched in the darkness. Betty sauntered to her cabin, head bowed, with what appeared to be an iron collar strapped to her neck. Along either side, right above her shoulders, was a bell that let out shrill rings with every stride. McLeary jumped as a loud voice called from behind him, "Enjoying the night, eh?"

He spun around and came face to face with Powell, who stood sipping a drink of his own. The planter cast him a tired smile, and his bloodshot eyes suggested that another drink or two would send him to bed.

"Sorry, McLeary." The planter chuckled. "I didn't mean to frighten you."

"Ain't yer fault, Henry," McLeary muttered, returning his gaze to the field.

"We got her all fixed up," Powell stated as he stepped beside him.

"Hmmm?"

"Betty."

"Oh."

After a brief silence, Powell said gently, "Don't harbor a guilty conscience, McLeary."

"It be that plain, ain't it?"

"Plain as day, I'm afraid," was the response. The planter took another sip and then remarked, "I didn't want to do it to her. I really didn't... but I can't have her running off on me again, you understand."

The farmer sighed. "I guess so."

"I'm making arrangements to have her sold off," he continued. "Well, trying to, that is."

"Whereabouts?"

"There's a trader down in Raleigh who's got his interest piqued," he said, "but between you and me, this fellow seems like trouble. Kind of reminds me of Buck in a way."

"How ye figure?"

"He treats his Negroes as if they grow off trees," Powell's voice was solemn, "or so I'm inclined to believe. After a while, you tend to find qualities among certain planters that are distasteful, to say the very least. This man says, and I quote, that he'll 'break her in quick enough.' He says every other word that'll come out of the nigger's mouth will be 'sir' or 'ma'am' by the time he's through with her. In this business, McLeary, you must take caution in everything you do. I am a respectable fellow, honest and decent, but some of these boys... well, they do more than give their hands a bruising. Take Buck, for instance. This fellow has done some wicked deeds: keeps his slaves cowering in fear all day, every day. I don't know what breed he's born of, but trust me when I say he's different than his father. His father would be rolling in his grave if he saw what's come of the place."

"Then why ye keep bringin' him back here?"

"I'm afraid of what will happen if I don't."

McLeary turned and saw a man who was disturbed, rocked to his core by an unspoken dread. He took a long sip from his drink and then let out a breath.

"Why don' ye turn yer back on all this, Henry?"

"What do you mean?"

"Why don' ye let 'em all go?"

"Free them, you mean?"

McLeary nodded.

"That wouldn't make much sense," Powell said, chuckling, but it was forced. "They're valuable commodities, every last one of them, and I have no desire seeing my fortunes crumble."

"But ain't whachya got 'spectable nuff?"

"This is what I was afraid of," the planter shook his head. "It seems to me, sir, that your act of charity has twisted your mind some. I'll tell you what though, I'll humor you. Let's say I free them all — where do you propose they run off to?"

"Well, er, up north, I reckon."

"To do what?"

The farmer shrugged. "How's I gonna know?"

"That's exactly my point," Powell answered. "They've got nothing, McLeary. *Nothing*. They're better off here, and if I may be so bold, sir, I urge you to stop reading abolitionist propaganda."

McLeary spoke up, careful not to let his voice rise too much. "I don' read none o' it."

"Then, respectfully," Powell's voice was tense, "quit telling me what to do with my slaves."

It was best to drop the subject altogether, McLeary decided. There was no sense in arguing with a man who was set in his ways. A long silence ensued, which the farmer interrupted by politely excusing himself and returning inside. Booth, who appeared lost in a haze, ventured past him at the door. They exchanged nods, but as McLeary was nearly out of earshot, a distant conversation suddenly roused his interest. He returned to the door, careful to remain unseen, and listened to the two voices.

Booth spoke first. "Did he take it?"

"I never suggested it to him," the planter replied. His voice dipped slightly, as if he was mindful of listening ears.

"Why not?"

130

"Let's just say that his intentions are incompatible with ours."

"Why do you figure that?"

"His heart's soft — he has sympathy for one of my slaves."

"Sympathy?" Booth scoffed. "I'll be damned..."

Silence.

"What's your next course of action?"

"To be frank with you, John, I'm not sure," Powell admitted. "Don't get me wrong, I'm concerned about this country's future as much as you are... but a conflict of such a great magnitude, as you suggest, is unfathomable."

"'Unfathomable' is hardly a word I would use to describe it," the other started. "Try *inevitable*. You've said it many times yourself, sir: there *will* be armed conflict if the federal government tries to dominate states. *Your* livelihood is at stake in this election, and as far as I see it, Lincoln will win it all."

"I share your pessimism to a degree," the planter said. "Lincoln poses a respectable challenge, I'll give him that, but he doesn't have enough support to win the electoral votes."

"Don't be so sure," was the response. "Think about it, Henry. The Democratic Party is fractured, and as long as there is no single candidate who can unify all of the southern states, Lincoln's guaranteed to win."

"John, I don't think you understand..."

"No, *you* don't understand," Booth interrupted, "if I may say so. Sir, this is a dire situation. *When* Lincoln wins, he'll begin to tighten the noose around everything you hold near and dear to your heart. You can kiss your life, your property, your *rights* goodbye if you choose not to act. Shady Grove may well be one of the first lines of defense against Washington, and you need to be ready. You *need* McLeary to provide the safehouse. Arms, munitions, supplies, anything that could help with the resistance — let him store it all in that barn of his. The fellow has spent the last sixty years living as a hermit, hasn't he? No one will suspect him of treachery."

"That may be easy for you to say," Powell countered, "but the man's stubborn. He may not take fondly to this request."

"That's where you come in," the other replied. "You've already wined and dined him — struck up friendly conversations. All you have to do now is ask him for this favor, and I'm sure he will oblige."

"Perhaps." The planter spoke uneasily. "Let's say he accepts. What do you suppose the plan is if he should get caught?"

"It won't be your problem. They'll probably arrest him, hang him, and during that time you'll be thanking the Lord that you were wise enough to put the risk on him."

"That's harsh, John, don't you think?"

"Maybe it is," he admitted, "but war is war. You should know that more than anyone, my friend. In a time of crisis, sacrifices often need to be made."

Powell fell silent.

"You're not a bad man, Henry," Booth said. "You're looking out for this town, and for your way of life. McLeary's time is past him — you've said so yourself. He doesn't have much left to gain in this world. It's only practical to have him be the scapegoat, should the need arise."

It was as if he suddenly awoke from a bad dream. McLeary studied his glass, which shook in his hand. The air had a certain repulsive quality that left his lips dry and parched. His knees buckled, and he pressed his free hand against the wall to steady himself.

His suspicions were confirmed — Powell *was* up to something. Now that he knew what that something was, he was ready to grab his wife by the wrist and hurry out of the place as quickly as his feet could move them.

Scapegoat...

The word tormented his thoughts, and the truth made his head pound and stomach queasy. He had never considered Powell a friend, but the nature of his intentions left him hurt and struggling to find an answer. An escape. He had suspected that the planter would eventually ask him for a favor, some small-handed deed, but to be the main cog in an operation in which he took all the risk... that was not to be taken lightly.

Given that he found their 'cause' and all it stood for to be more and more repulsive by the second, he was half-tempted to march out there and slug them both. The sting went away as quickly as it came, and anger took its place. If Powell wanted to play games with him, it was a pity he had neglected to study his opponent.

Ye take me for a fool, ain't ye, Henry? McLeary fumed. *Yer gonna git whut's comin' to ye.*

Powell and Booth made their way inside after a few minutes and disappeared into the dark halls. They were oblivious to the old farmer, who pressed his back against the wall and concealed himself in darkness. When footsteps ceased and the room grew silent, McLeary slipped out to the back porch. He gazed upon the sprawling field, which glowed gently beneath pale moonlight. The slave quarters stood silent and undisturbed, and with any luck it would remain that way. Against his better judgement, against every bell and whistle in his head that pleaded otherwise, he knew what his next move needed to be.

***

He made like hell towards the cabins. In spite of his age, his legs were nimble and spry, and they carried him quickly across the field. He propped himself against the side of the nearest structure and immersed himself in the shadows. The walls hummed gently, and from the rustling that sounded from within, the evening was winding down. A small window stood merely feet away from him, and from it seeped a flickering orange light. McLeary crept over to it and peeked inside.

It was a small room, cramped and confined, that hosted a quaint scene. Over a dozen slaves of all ages went about their business calmly and without care; it was a striking contrast to their busy work in the fields. A gentle fire crackled in an old hearth, which brought a soothing warmth to the occupants. In a corner of the room, women were busy scrubbing dishes and cleaning up what was left of their supper. A small collection of toys lay scattered around in the center as children indulged in their fantasies. The men sat at ease by the fire, some positioned on the floor and others sprawled upon cots. A few noises rang out: the clanging of pots and pans, children squealing with delight, fathers snoozing away after a hard day's work. The cabin had a simplistic charm that resonated fondly with McLeary. How nice it was to enjoy simple, leisurely moments, where there were no worries or unwanted interruptions. More and more, it seemed like the world was devoid of such pleasures.

He hurried past the window and ventured towards the next cabin. More late-night leisure. How exactly he would proceed in his venture was lost to him, but if there was one certainty, it was that he needed to remain hidden at all costs. After all, he was only here for one reason, rather, one *person*... From cabin to cabin, the old farmer cast a glance in each one, searching for the woman with melancholy eyes and tear-stained cheeks. His efforts proved futile until he looked into the final cabin.

The room was smaller than the others, dark and neglected. Only a sliver of moonlight seeped into a space that was plagued by stale air and a bitter chill. It was entirely deprived of furnishings, save for a tiny wooden chair upon which the woman was propped. She sat in the far corner, head bowed in what appeared to be a restless sleep. It was the way in which her head and shoulders sank, McLeary concluded, that shook him to his core. Within her was a spirit so battered and broken that it was better off not living at all. Through the pale fog, the farmer made out what appeared to be iron shackles clamped around her wrists. He cast one final glance towards the other cabins, and upon seeing that the coast was clear, he hurried into the room.

The floorboards groaned under his shoes, which stirred the young woman from her sleep. Wide eyes lit up with pure terror at the sight of him, but before she could make a sound, McLeary rushed over to her and cupped a hand around her mouth.

"Keep quiet, Betty," the farmer whispered, raising a finger to his lips. "I's gettin' ye outta here."

A startled look flickered across her face, but it was brief. Her frightened eyes locked upon him, and McLeary spoke again. "Listen here," he said, "ye gotta tell me how's to free ye. Ain't there a key or somethin'?"

Her gaze shifted from him slightly, much to his surprise. It focused upon something past him towards the door. McLeary's blood ran cold as he turned around...

A young slave, no more than twenty years of age, stood in the doorway with folded arms. He was large and barrel-chested, and he eyed him angrily. "Ye ain't s'pposed te be here, suh." He spoke slowly. "Wuh business ye got comin' down here?"

McLeary scrambled for an answer. "I struck a deal wit' yer master," the farmer's tone clipped the air. "Betty be *mine* now. Go on 'n' gimme the key."

The slave's eyes narrowed upon him like a predator, and his stance grew wide. "Lemme go 'n' git Misstuh Powell." His tone was cold and bitter. "I ain't lettin' her go till I hear from de mas'r hisself."

"Ye be wantin' me to tell him yer gettin' uppity wit' me, boy?" McLeary challenged, glaring at him. "Gimme the key or yer gonna be the next one in chains."

He stood frozen for what seemed like an eternity. Only the chill breeze scurried through the air. Slowly, reluctantly, the slave sauntered over to him and fished out the key from his pocket. After being told to make his way back to his cabin or 'the devil's gonna come after ye,' the slave shot him a glare and left. With sweat pouring down his neck, McLeary frantically removed the cuffs from Betty's wrists and hoisted her to her feet.

"Let's git ye outta here," he murmured and made his way quickly towards the door.

"Why's ya helpin' me?" the voice called softly from behind him.

"Ye got a boy to find, ain't ye?"

She nodded slowly, tears streaming down her cheeks. The farmer shot a glance down the row of cabins: All clear. He turned his head in the other direction where, at the far end of the field, a thin line of trees marked the beginnings of a dense forest. He waved for Betty to come to him and pointed towards the trees. "I ain't goin' wit' ye, Betty, ye understan'," McLeary stated. "But go on in them woods yonder 'n' keep movin' as fast as ye can."

She nodded once more, and before she ventured out on her own, she wrapped her arms around him and squeezed tightly. The farmer's heart raced, but he found that he could breathe easier. A choice had been made, and he would sleep well knowing that it was the right one. He gave her a pat on the back, and without a second to waste, she ran towards the green horizon.

That was enough company for one year, let alone one night. All the pointless banter, jovial songs, it was enough to drive him crazy. He wanted to turn in for the night, a wish that could not come soon enough.

Buck stood on the back porch, arms folded across his chest. The moonlight cast its glow upon the field, and with dark eyes that harbored a raging storm, he carefully surveyed the property.

At the far end of the field, he spotted the dark blur. A moving figure, human enough, disturbed the still landscape. His eyes narrowed and he took several steps forward until the tips of his shoes touched the grass.

She was a woman, plain enough. A Negro woman. Her hair danced in the wind as she raced towards…

Buck's eyes grew wide.

"Sunnovabitch," he gasped, then louder, "*Goddamn sunnovabitch*!"

He spun around and sprinted back into the house. There would be hell to pay…

Chapter 8

Philadelphia, Pennsylvania
July 9, 1860

It was a hot flash that came upon him. Streicher sat among his colleagues in the main room of the office. The air was stale and dry; sweat glistened across his brow and ran along the back of his neck. Blistering heat lingered, leaving him light-headed and craving a cold drink. The summer months were the most unbearable, and this particular occasion left him even worse for wear.

Doyle had called for an impromptu meeting, in which the *Freedom Fightin' Firebrands* would see to it that justice was brought down 'swift and true.' Throughout the week, the Irishman had boasted about his victory over his adversary, and he had called upon Streicher to serve as his witness. The men had bolstered his pride by offering congratulatory remarks and pats on the back, but it was all too obvious that their gestures were ingenuine. It seemed that the rest of them were like Streicher — only working to collect a paycheck. Nothing more.

Doyle had ordered them to 'torch' Hill's business with their words, and before long it seemed as if their work was entirely devoted towards toppling his reputation. Streicher quickly found himself scathing Hill, denouncing him in one instance as 'the southern planter's mistress.' Although his labors often left him with an uneasy stomach and a gnawing guilt, he also took pleasure (admittedly so) in hurling slurs and ridicules at the man who barred the woman he loved from him. He had no need to fret, he reminded himself; his pen was anonymous. Doyle's name was the one attached to such slanderous accusations.

They sat around and gazed upon their boss with silent concern. His face was so flushed and sweat-soaked that it appeared he would succumb to the heat at any moment. But Doyle's smile was wide, and his voice was loaded with triumph.

"Now, we've got a good one here, lads," the Irishman declared, waving a paper in his hand. "A rebuttal from Mr. Half-Wit. Allow me the pleasure of reading to you such a grand manifesto from a man whose breeches are three sizes too large."

He cleared his voice, eyed his audience with a smug grin, and proceeded to read the letter:

"*Dear Mr Doyle,*

Strong men are driven by their convictions — who does this chap think he is? Shakespeare? — *and I warn you that I am compelled to take action. Your defamations against my name are downright* <u>*heinous*</u>

and _appalling_. I will have you know that my business is of a reputable nature, and I provide quality products to the gentlemen of this city. Ah, yes, Mr Hill, I stand corrected — your products are quality enough for rats to defecate upon.

My associates garner as much respect as I do — sure, they're scum too — *and it disgusts me to know that you treat them with the same indignation. They are _honest_ businessmen, worthy of any praise they receive, and they stand for an institution that has propelled this country to prosperous heights.* 'Prosperous heights,' eh? They can tell that to their starving, overworked Negroes.

Let it be known that there is a coalition against you, sir. You have stoked enough fires that they are now blazing out of control, and you can be assured that _you_ will burn because of it. Gee, how long do you think it took him to come up with *that* sentence? *Be warned that there will be consequences for your words, and it is too late to make amends.*

This conflict will be put to rest _swiftly_ and _decisively_, and I will enjoy reducing your name to _ashes_.

Signed — the one and very only — *Mr. Robert Hill*."

Doyle's smile rivaled the glow of the sun, and as he cast one last glance at the paper, he shook his head slowly.

"Well, Mr. Hill," the Irishman met the gaze of his workers, many of whom were glassy-eyed, lost in their own thoughts, "here is my rebuttal to your rebuttal…" With the paper held high, he tore it to pieces and let the remnants fall to the floor. His audience sat in silence, unfazed by their boss's action.

But Streicher's heart raced. The letter sounded like a threat more than anything else, and if there was anyone who was not to be trifled with, it was Robert Hill. Doyle was playing a dangerous game…

"Lads, we have ourselves a pest unlike any other," the Irishman stated. "No man threatens my business and walks away unscathed. Being the pampered snob that he is, I can guarantee that Mr. Hill's words are nothing more than just that. *However*… this bloke has bit off more than he can chew, and by God, we will give him something to *feast* upon.

Unless I say otherwise, every word, every sentence, every article we publish must blast that greedy scamp until he's drowning in his own filth. Put the rope around him; put the rope around his 'associates.' I want to make certain that any scoundrel in this city who profits from southern plantations has sleepless nights. Men like Hill cannot be negotiated with, and quite frankly, what's the sense? They're vile degenerates, every last one of them, and we need to hit them harder than ever before."

Doyle fired away orders and the office was suddenly jumping with activity. Streicher made his way to his desk and slumped in his chair. The task was nothing out of the ordinary: denounce Hill's business as a 'sleazy, deplorable operation that fills the pockets of heartless misers.' He sat at his desk throughout the day, not so much as placing the pen in his grip. There was something unwelcoming about the day. Words of conviction were penned by Mr. Hill, and any man who was wise enough to heed the warning would have done so long ago. His 'coalition,' whoever they were, were likely as infuriated as he was... and there was bound to be a response.

As the day came to an end, Doyle popped into his office, and at the sight of an empty desk and blank pages, he frowned. "Having trouble making some progress, eh, lad?"

"I guess so," Streicher shrugged.

"Hmm..." Doyle eyed him carefully. "You don't look so good. What's got you down?"

"Nothing, sir."

"I know you're lying to me. Come now, lad, out with it..."

Streicher sighed. The truth had been buried for so long that eventually it was destined to surface. Albeit reluctantly, he began to speak... "I have doubts, sir."

"Doubts?" Doyle asked. "About what?"

"About what we stand for."

"What do you mean?"

"This feud with Hill..." Streicher's voice faltered slightly. "I mean, it's coming to an ugly head, and there may be consequences for what we've said."

"Now, lad," the other said, chuckling, "I know you're smarter than this. Don't start believing something that isn't true. Hill's all talk…"

"So are we…"

"We're working towards something that's greater than ourselves — that's not talk. That's action. There aren't enough people in this country who will fight for the abolitionist cause, and that's why our message needs to pack a hard punch."

"But do you truly believe in it?"

"Believe in what? Abolition?"

"Yes."

"Well, of course! Don't you?"

"Can't say that I do, sir." He could not believe the words that were coming out of his mouth.

"Are you sick in the head or something?" Doyle's tone grew firm. "After working here all this time, you mean to tell me you *don't* believe in what we're doing?"

"With all due respect, sir, we're agitating people — nothing more."

"As well we should," Doyle protested. "Any man who stands for such an appalling institution as slavery should be stripped of everything he owns."

"Have you ever been to a plantation?"

"What?"

"Have you ever been to a plantation?"

"Well, no…"

"Neither have I."

"What difference does that make?"

"How can we fight against something, sir, that we know nothing about?"

"We know *everything* about it, and what a vile business it is…"

"How can you say that with certainty?"

"Because I've been told…"

"Word of mouth isn't enough."

"What's gotten into you today, Streicher?"

"I'm only trying to bring some perspective to the situation before it escalates any further," he replied. "Hill's going to be at our throats, and we need to make amends before anyone gets hurt."

"I beat the man's ass!" Doyle cried out. "For God's sake, what's the worst thing he'd do to us?"

"I'm not sure, sir," was the response, "and that's what I'm afraid of."

"There's no chance that I would *ever* back down to him, I'll tell you that right now."

"Why not?"

"Where I'm from, any man who has his wits about him doesn't run away from a scrap."

"That's exactly my point…"

"What is?"

"This façade of yours, or whatever you want to call it," Streicher went on, "it's exactly that. It's not real. Sure, you can say all the right things. You can denounce this or that; you can cry out every injustice until you're blue in the face. But it makes not one bit of difference if you don't believe in what you stand for."

"I'll have you know, boy," Doyle said, pointing a finger at him, "that I practice what I preach. I treat a Negro man the same as a white man. And I don't bat an eye about it."

"I've never seen you talk to a Negro."

"That's because you're not around me every bloody second of the day."

"Be that as it may," Streicher countered, "I've seen you walk up and down these streets. If a Negro walks by, you don't share the sidewalk with him; you make him walk in the street."

"Are you calling me a damn hypocrite?"

Streicher fell silent.

"You are." Doyle nodded as his eyes flickered with rage. "I can't believe this. Streicher, you'd best keep your trap shut…"

"But am I wrong, sir?"

"Piss off…"

"You didn't answer my question."

"Piss off!"

"There's nothing to be ashamed of, sir…"

"Ashamed?" Doyle let out a laugh and threw his hands in the air. "Heavens, no, I'm not ashamed. *Irritated*, now there's a word you could use…"

"But you don't deny it."

"For Christ's sake, would you shut up about it already?"

"You know I'm right."

"Negroes deserve to be equal, Streicher."

"No, they *don't*!" the young writer cried out. "And we need to quit acting like they *should* be! You don't believe it, and neither do I. If you want the truth, the *real* truth, I think you started this business for one reason: to piss and moan on everyone else. Well, guess what? You've started one hell of a fire, and it's probably one that's too big for you to stop. So, before things get out of hand — I *implore* you, sir — apologize to Mr Hill. Let's stop this thing before any more fists start flying…"

Doyle stood frozen, his face so red that it mirrored Hell itself. A quivering jaw and curled fists made Streicher's breath grow short. What the hell was he thinking speaking to his boss in such a way? Did he have some sort of a death wish?

But then a switch flipped…

Slowly, steadily, the color fled Doyle's cheeks, and he started to laugh. Louder and louder, the laughter erupted from him in short, erratic bursts until he was bent over at the waist. The jovial thunder shook the walls, and he gazed upon Streicher with tear-filled eyes.

"You bastard," Doyle choked out, wagging another finger at him. "You sly bastard. You nearly had me there for a moment…"

The realization hit Streicher suddenly, and he tried to join in on the fun. But his laughter was short and forced.

"Damn, son," Doyle remarked, clapping his hands. "For a kraut, you not only have a sense of humor — you

have a rather demented one at that. My kind of a guy!"
Streicher jumped as a hand came down hard upon his
shoulder. "Well done, lad!" Doyle applauded him.
"Way to get the blood going before the end of the day."

"Er, uh…" he stammered. "All in fun, sir."

"Can't wait to get home and tell the wife about this
one," Doyle said as the tears continued to flow down his
cheeks. "Christ almighty, she'll be beside herself."

"Right, sir."

"You know how to get a good laugh out of me, lad.
For a second there, I was ready to kick your keister
across the street."

"I guess I got you good then." Streicher spoke
softly, trying to collect his breath.

"Damn right!" Doyle gave him another slap on the
back. "Well done, boy. Now, if you'd be so kind, I'd
rather you take it easy on me and let me get home for
the night."

"Of course, sir."

They exchanged goodbyes and the Irishman fled
the office. Streicher let out a long breath and slumped in
his chair. His clothes were drenched in sweat.

Idiot, he scolded himself. *Were you out of your
mind?*

As he locked up for the night, all too eager to put
the day behind him, a shrill voice rang out.

"Sir!"

He jumped in his boots and spun around, only to
find the postman hurrying towards him. A letter was

clutched high in the air as his satchel swung with each stride.

"Can I help you?" Streicher asked.

"Sorry, sir." He panted heavily and extended the letter towards him. "I wanted to get this to you before you closed shop. Looks like it slipped through the cracks…"

Streicher glanced at what was written on the envelope and smiled.

Erich.

***

In the comfort of his room, all the worries of the world disappeared. He was protected from harmful elements, harsh realities that seemed all the more encroaching and disruptive with each passing day. Streicher threw himself upon his bed, and it groaned irritably upon impact. It was a cramped room, much like his office: old, shabby, and in dire need of a fresh coat of paint. The cracked white walls were cheap and hollow. In the summer, it was like an oven, and even cool night air did little to bring about any comfort.

But it mattered little to Streicher, who was focused upon something else entirely. His hands shook as he feverishly tore open the envelope and held the letter in front of him. The day had been eventful, to say the least, but even in its waning hours, there was still promise. As the moon cast its glow through a broken window, he strained his eyes and began to read:

Dear Erich,

Every morning, I open my curtains to sunny skies and tranquil gardens. As the summer blesses us with its natural beauty, I grow envious of those who enjoy the blessings of life's simplest moments. There are dreams of mine that I dearly wish would become realities, where you and I find peace underneath a shady tree, or by a quiet pond. Summer's light offers as much promise as it does every year, yet I cannot help but be laden with melancholy. We are so close, not so much as a stone's throw away, yet our worlds could not drive us further apart.

Father has hardly spoken to me since his encounter with Mr. Doyle. I dare not mention your name when I am in his presence, as I fear it may push him to lengths that I dare not wish to witness. Lately, he has kept himself locked away in his study, and it may be that his tolerance of Mr. Doyle has reached its end. I try to stay hidden in my room, but I cannot help hearing the voices next door. I am unsure who the voices belong to, but it is clear enough that they are southern men. Often times, they are careful to keep their mouths hushed. Such secretive dealings leave me with a sinking feeling in my stomach. It would be in Mr. Doyle's best interest to look out for himself.

There is a storm brewing, one that may very well be too great to control. These men who visit Father are driven by anger, and what little I can make of their discourse is enough to keep me awake at night. I hear whispers of their schemes. They threaten violence and retaliation against those who oppose them.

More and more, I fear that hostilities have run too deep among too many people, and old wounds can no longer be healed. What is to become of our country if such division should persist? I am a God-fearing woman, and the thought of carnage tears away at my heart. What will you do if men with such uncompromising convictions should confront you?

Please, make the right choice. We have a future to look after. There is a life for us after the storm, whenever it should end, and we must continue to remain patient. I beg of you to stay away from the violence, should it come to your door. Do not allow such passions and hatred fill your heart as they do the hearts of other men. You are a far better person than they are.

It is my sincerest hope that this note finds its way to you. We are too young to have to face such overwhelming obstacles, but our love must triumph through it all. Remain tender and compassionate in the wake of hardship, and know that my love for you is as strong now as it has ever been. I will rejoice on the day when we can begin a new life together. Until then, have faith in God's perfect timing.

Love,

He delicately placed the letter aside and rubbed his eyes. Though sincere, her words reflected a certain lack of understanding about the way of the world. Not that she could be blamed, of course. Any person blessed enough to be born into a life of such privilege and luxury hardly needed to fret about the outside world. To a certain point, he shared her concern: Doyle needed to keep his mouth shut, and being on the receiving end of anything Hill and his 'associates' threw at him would prove damaging to his reputation and business — and yes, he could very well end up with a black eye in the process (which, quite honestly, would be well-deserved). But he could not grasp her grave warnings, which as far as Streicher was concerned, were unrealistic… or so he hoped.

The more he thought about it, the more he came to the conclusion that the men Hill did business with were likely self-serving opportunists — nothing more. They would not dare to use extreme violence against Doyle or anyone else who was employed by the *Freedom Fightin' Firebrands*. Acting upon their emotions, were they so deep and misguided, would have landed them behind bars. Yet there was something more about the letter that kept his interest. He picked it up and skimmed it again…

'What is to become of our country if such division should persist?' 'What will you do if men with such

uncompromising convictions should confront you?'
Streicher could not help but shake his head and chuckle.
Easy does it, Emma, he thought. *No need to fret over nonsense.*

Sure, there were Shane Doyles out there, but their numbers were small. Most men were pragmatic and good-hearted. Violence would never erupt on such a large scale as she seemed to suggest.

Niggers and Lincoln — they're not worth the trouble one way or another. Whether slavery expanded westward, it did not matter. Whether Lincoln was elected, it did not matter. Indeed, Streicher could not help but feel his blood boil at the thoughts of such controversies. Why did *any* of it matter? All that anyone could ask for was that they had food on the table every day and went to sleep every night in a warm bed.

Before long, he made his way under the covers and spent the night tossing and turning. It appeared that his thoughts — the nagging pests that they were — could not be ignored. For as much as he tried to free his mind of worry, it always returned with a vengeance. Haunting sounds rang out in his sleep: cannon thunder, gunfire, guttural cries…

When he woke up the next morning, he was drenched in sweat. As he dressed himself for the work day, the truth hit him quick and hard.

Don't try to fool yourself, Erich…

Slavery. It mattered — its future and everything it stood for (although what exactly it stood for remained a mystery to him).

Lincoln. He mattered — if he gained control of the White House, there would be uproar from southern states. Possibly (no, *probably*) armed defiance.

Whatever 'storm' was to come upon the country, as Emma suggested, would be grim and cruel. He hated to admit it, but there was a real reason to worry.

Perhaps the dream of a new life with his bride-to-be was to be crushed by a greater force, one which was out of their control. Streicher sighed as he laced his shoes and strode out into the street.

God willing, the storm would pass quickly...

***

In the distance, it was a dark haze. A cloud of black lingering among what was otherwise a clear blue sky. As he made his way through busy streets, Streicher did not care to dwell much upon the strange happening that the new day presented. Yet as he came around every street corner and bend in the road, a strong odor lingered. Smoke. He focused his eyes upon the wisps of darkness, which loomed nearer to him with every stride.

Almost instinctively, his heart raced and his pace quickened. He needed answers — rather, assurance. Fast. Assurance that the numbing fear that overcame him was only a work of his imagination. But as he came

upon what was once the home of the *Freedom Fightin'*
Firebrands, he nearly fainted at the sight.

The old wooden structure, which had stood proud
for so long as a symbol of newfound freedom and ideals,
had been reduced to a pile of charred rubble. Thick
black smoke poured out from the heap of fresh ashes. A
large crowd gathered to witness the devastation,
marking the grim aftermath of what had been a blazing
fire. Teams of firefighters milled about the scene and
doused the remnants with buckets of water.

A lump forced its way into Streicher's throat as he
found himself sprinting towards the commotion. It was
the work of nightmares, a chilling reality that left far
more questions than answers. Unfathomable, it truly
was, how merely hours prior he had closed the door on
what was the final day of work, entirely ignorant of
what was to come. His breath grew short as the
questions began flooding into his head…

Dear God, was it something I've done? I
remembered to blow out all the candles before I left,
didn't I? I checked all the rooms too, right?

He approached several of his co-workers, whose
faces were equally pale and grief-stricken. They stood
huddled together and looked upon him with twinkling
eyes.

"When did this happen?"

"Overnight, apparently," one of them answered
solemnly. "A few folks said this place lit up the night
sky."

"To do that kind of damage," Streicher said, gazing upon the wreckage, "it must've been one hell of a blaze."

"That's putting it lightly…"

"Where's Doyle?" All of them stiffened, their complexions sinking to a sicklier grey. "He's not here?"

"Oh, he's here alright," another voice chimed in and pointed towards the portly mound of a man who sat upon his knees in front of his smoldering shrine.

"Has he said anything?"

"Not a word."

My God…

He approached his boss with slow, cautious steps, but was met with no acknowledgement. Instead, Doyle's eyes remained locked upon his lost sanctuary, and a fire burned in them that was unlike anything Streicher had ever seen before.

"Sir," the young man began, "I swear to you, I locked up the same way I do any other night. The candles, they were all blown out before I left; I'm sure of it. In all honesty, I don't have the faintest idea what could have caused this."

Silence. A raw tension filled the air, and the only sounds he heard were the pops of dying embers. Streicher was about to step away when the Irishman's voice, low and deep, drifted to his ears. "This was not caused by some force of nature," Doyle responded, "or a random accident."

"Sir?"

With his eyes still teetering between despair and rage, the Irishman handed him a note. Streicher's eyes widened at what was written.

'*Abolition burns with its martyrs.*'

"I found it folded on my doorstep this morning."

"Have you told the authorities about this, sir?"

"No need," Doyle muttered. "Justice will be served soon enough."

For the first time, the Irishman's words carried malice. A lust for revenge that would only be satisfied by an extreme response. If there was one certainty to be found, it was that retaliation was inevitable. There would be hell to pay...

Chapter 9

There was silence in the great mansion. What had once been a place of liveliness and commotion was suddenly as still and eerie as a grave. Henry Powell sat in the parlor room and twirled a cigar in between his fingers, occasionally bringing it to his lips and letting out long, slow breaths. It had been a week of sleepless nights and constant worries, but by the end of it, his problems had been put to rest... for the most part.

The night Betty ran off, he and his companions had scrambled for their horses and raced into the woods after her. Their search had come up empty, much to the planter's dismay. Day after day, they traversed the countryside, asking neighbors and local officials if they had seen the fugitive slave. Powell was left without answers for five days until he received a letter from Richmond authorities saying that she had been found by a patrolman, tangled in heavy brush, near Virginia's southern border. When the ordeal was sorted out and Betty was returned to her owner, the search party had disbanded and Powell's friends returned to their home states.

What proved to be more worrisome was not necessarily the escape itself, but rather the root of it. Silas, his trusted overseer, had informed him that a white man ventured into the cabin and claimed he had purchased Betty. The man was apparently dressed up 'all good-like,' undoubtedly an attendee at the party. His face was 'stern-lookin', ain't one I's willin' to mess wit',' and he had a grey beard that 'ain't done up too good.' Powell mulled over the description, trying to piece together a puzzle that did not quite fit. Buck had not seen anyone by the cabins, and neither did any of the other slaves. Then it hit him one night as sudden as a bolt of lightning.

McLeary.

He was not present for the search. In fact, he had disappeared entirely from the party and had not bothered to even share a word with him in the following days. No letter. No knock on the door. And he was the only guest present that night who could have possibly known who Betty was.

Powell took another draw and shook his head slowly. He should have known that the farmer was too dangerous to form an acquaintance with, let alone a friendship. There was too much sympathy in his heart — he had showed it plainly enough when he had brought Betty to his doorstep only days prior to her second escape. At the very least, the puzzle was quickly becoming solved, and all that was needed was confirmation. And there was only one source who could provide him with that information…

He gazed up at the young woman who stood before him. Her dress was torn and smeared in mud. Long scratches ran along her arms and legs, and her dark hair was a tangled mess. For as much stress and aggravation that she had caused him, the planter admittedly could not help but take pity on her. Her brown eyes trembled, but no tears were shed. She stood firm, almost defiant, and he secretly admired her bravery. It was bound to happen, or so it seemed, that she would run off again. There was a spirit in her that, though battered and bruised, could not be broken. And he did not care to do any more damage to her. All that was needed was a simple answer…

"Betty." Powell spoke gently. "We can make this really easy on ourselves…"

Her eyes were fixed to the floor, but the planter paid it no mind. He took another puff and continued, "I can take you down to Atlanta. Perhaps there's a kind owner who would be willing to acquire your services, and you may be granted an opportunity to find your son."

Silence.

"The price for such a future, should you be interested, is providing me with the answer to one question: who freed you that night?"

Again, silence prevailed. The planter shifted in his chair. One way or another, she would be sold far away

161

from Virginia. Far away from where she could ever return to his plantation. She was the reason he kept a revolver buried in his nightstand. She was the reason he woke up each morning in a cold sweat. And she was the reason he began to question his own conscience, a troubling habit that he desperately needed to abandon. His lips grew dry as he fought for his words.

"I suggest you cooperate," he urged her. "Betty, be thankful that I'm your master. If you dared to run off on any other plantation, you'd have likely found yourself whipped, beaten, or branded. Some boys might've even sent you to your grave. But I am a man of character, you see, and not only do I value my investments, I value decency and goodwill even more. So, do me a favor just this once, if you'd please — name me the man who freed you from your chains."

Silence.

Powell took another puff and said, "I don't enjoy chaining you down like some mule. The truth is I'd rather have you in here cooking supper, but you have to prove your worth. And ever since you've been here, the only thing you've proven to me is that you're not worth the trouble to keep. That can all change, however, if you choose to straighten up. Now, I'll ask again, who freed you?"

She stood frozen, not daring to speak. Not daring to suggest that she even had a pulse...

"Was it McLeary — yes or no?"

Silence.

"Betty, yes or no?"

Silence.

"Betty…"

"Yes."

The word came as softly as a passing breeze, but it was clear enough. Powell nodded slowly, the wheels of his mind churning, as gentle sobs were heard above him. The young woman buried her face in her hands and proceeded to weep. It mattered little to him though. He had received his answer, and that was enough. One last loose end needed to be tied… "You're free, Betty."

His own words startled him. The house suddenly seemed quieter than it had ever been before, and he quickly glanced over his shoulder to watch out for prying eyes. There were none, as far as he could tell, and he reclined in his chair. For the first time, Betty lowered her hands and met his gaze with large, tear-filled eyes. Her brow raised at the news, as if she could hardly make any sense of it.

"Ye ain't serious?" she whispered.

"I am," Powell nodded, still surprised by what was spewing out of his mouth. "Give me some time to prepare the necessary documentation, and before noon tomorrow, you'll be a free woman. But I need a promise, you hear, that you won't say a word about this to anyone. Do you understand?"

She nodded her head.

"Very good then." Powell put the cigar to his lips and inhaled deeply. "I'll have Sampson escort you back to your quarters. You understand that your... *accommodations* will not be very comfortable, given your most recent escapade."

"Ain't gonna worry me none, suh." She shook her head. "Morrow I's a free woman, and I's gonna go 'n' find ma son."

"I wish you all the best, truly I do."

Powell felt a wave of relief overcome him as they parted for the night, but it was brief. His chips were placed into a game that was becoming too risky for his liking. Placing trust in Betty was the last thing he could have ever dreamed of doing, but her freedom needed to be granted. She had tormented his thoughts for too long, and although his wife would vehemently disapprove, he did not care. He wanted her gone..

But before those preparations were put in order, there was a far more pressing matter to address first. Thomas McLeary had wronged him in such a way that sent the blood scurrying through his veins. *He* was the real threat, not Betty... and such a threat needed to be stopped. Immediately. Powell extinguished his cigar and leapt to his feet. He knew what he needed to do.

***

McLeary cracked a smile as he rested his head upon the pillow. The moon's soft glow flickered through the curtains, and the soothing breeze of a calm night brought safety and comfort. For the first time in over a week, he came to bed with a quiet mind. It had been too long without word of capture; Betty must have slipped past unnoticed and was well on her way towards Georgia. It had been a dangerous gamble, to say the least, but it had most certainly paid off. The old farmer chuckled and rolled over on his side. Maybe there was a God after all.

His wife slept quietly beside him, lost in her dreams. Alice had never suffered a hard day in her life, or so he was convinced. It was her carefree spirit and optimism that McLeary admired. She rarely harbored any grievances or worries. But at the same time, she was also often gullible...

Her trust may have been taken advantage of during the party, McLeary could not deny. Just as word of a runaway slave spread among the guests, and men darted past one another in fits of panic and frenzy, the old farmer informed his wife that he had suddenly 'come down wit' a nasty bugger.' He must have made a convincing scene because his wife shot him a look of dire concern and when she placed a hand upon his forehead, the two of them made like mad towards their carriage. They barreled through the front door unseen, lost in the midst of the chaos. Powell had not as much as caught a whiff of them and they were gone... and that allowed McLeary to breathe easier on the ride home.

The following nights had not been as forgiving. Haunting visions tormented McLeary, grim possibilities that he desperately wished would only be the work of

165

his imagination. He dreamed that Betty was alone to fend for herself, and although her spirit was strong and determination unwavering, her capture threatened to break her entirely. As hours turned into days, and time ticked away with no word of her whereabouts, it seemed that her escape had been a success. There was no need to fret — not anymore. Best of all, Powell was none the wiser about *his* involvement, which filled his spirit with a childlike joy. He had restored the hope of a broken woman, and a narcissistic louse was left wallowing in his sorrow. A more perfect outcome could not be envisioned.

His blissful rest was interrupted by a dull tapping. Soft and steady, it crept to his ears like a gentle buzz. He propped himself to his elbows, careful not to disturb his wife, and listened closely.

Tap. Tap… Tap. Tap…

Yes, it was clear enough. It came from the front door. McLeary frowned as he threw off the covers and placed his feet on the floor. Whoever was at their door had better have a good reason for visiting at such an untimely hour. He slid on a pair of overalls and put on a fresh cotton shirt. Before leaving the room, he glanced at his wife. She lay still under the covers, undisturbed.

Good, he nodded. *Rest easy, hon.*

He swung the door open to find Powell at his doorstep. The planter's burly frame was etched in the pale moonlight, and there was something about him that made McLeary's hands sweaty. He was dressed up well enough, sporting his usual grey suit and hat, but minor flaws were apparent. One or two buttons were undone on his jacket. His tie clung sloppily to the side. Wisps of grey hair stuck out in random spots. Maybe it was a trick of the moonlight, but his complexion was sickly pale. Bloodshot eyes were sunken and glassy.

Lord almighty, McLeary thought. Had the man not rested since the party?

"Forgive me for disturbing you at such a terrible time, McLeary," Powell's voice was weak and tired, "but it would appear that I am a man of unfortunate circumstance."

"Ain't nothin' to be sorry for, Henry." McLeary waved a hand. "Whut be the treble?"

Powell turned and pointed down the road. "I was returning from an outing in Richmond," he began and added with a half-hearted smirk, "one of those late-night extravaganzas. High society crowds, you know — a real wine and cheese affair. Anyway, my horses spotted something down yonder — must've been a fox or something of that nature, and suddenly they're running around like they're possessed. They're jostling the carriage about this way and that, and the next thing I know I've got two missing horses and a carriage that's tangled in a heap of thick brush. I was hoping that you'd be able to help me free the carriage for the time being. I'll have to return for it in the morning."

"Oh, er, sure thang, Henry," McLeary said. "Show me where it be 'n' we'll get it up 'n' outta there."

McLeary grabbed a lantern and the two of them plunged into the darkness. Crickets chirped in the blackness, and the soft whisper of the wind came to their ears. It was a silent night. Calm. There was nothing out of the ordinary, and yet McLeary felt a sinking feeling in the pit of his stomach. There was something about Powell that seemed... off. His words were a bit too refined, polished, especially given the alleged circumstances. Any man who experienced such an abrupt accident was sure to be stuttering and fumbling over his words. Sure, the planter looked as if it had been a mess of a night, but his smooth tongue suggested otherwise.

Powell's voice came to his ears. "This month has plagued me with something terrible," he remarked. "For one reason or another, it seems I can't take care of my own property. Betty was the first to run off on me, and now the horses. Who's next to go? My wife?"

McLeary fell silent, and the lantern shook in his hand.

"You heard the news about Betty, didn't you, McLeary?"

"'Fraid so."

"I do apologize, sir, there was so much commotion that night that I had no time to say goodbye to you and the Mrs."

"Don' worry none."

"Well, quite truthfully, it seems like all I do these days is worry. It's been over a week now and there's still no sign of the girl. For her sake, I hope she's got enough know-how to survive. She wasn't a cheap commodity either, if you remember. That's all I need is for my Negroes to start thinking they can run for the hills."

Silence.

Powell gestured down a narrow path and led them further into the darkness. The orange glow from the lantern illuminated tall trees, thick bushes, and buzzing gnats. The farmer's heart pounded as they ventured further and further into the undergrowth. For some reason, the night air had a sort of strange repulsive quality about it. He should have never bothered to answer the door…

They parted low-hanging limbs and crowded brush as they made their way to a large clearing. McLeary squinted and gazed at the far end…

There was the carriage, rested comfortably at the base of a tall tree. It looked clean and untouched, having taken not even a scratch of damage. Then he surveyed the front of it. Two horses sat comfortably in the grass, taking pleasure in the comfort that came with a quiet night. Their reins were tied to the trunk. McLeary heard a click and suddenly his heart sank.

Powell spun around to face him. A silver revolver glistened in the white light, and the barrel cast its menacing gaze upon him. McLeary staggered backwards a few steps, desperately trying to maintain his footing. The planter stood frozen, his eyes sparked by a restless rage.

"Henry…"

"Don't." Powell's voice shook and he held up a hand. "McLeary, if you have *any* brains about you, I suggest you keep quiet."

The farmer obeyed.

"I welcomed you into my home." The planter's icy tone pierced the air. "I gave you food, drinks, treated you as a dear friend. And your way of saying 'thank you' is to sneak away and free one of my slaves?"

"H-Henry, I ain't…"

"Betty confessed everything to me."

"Huh?"

"She's been caught, McLeary," Powell stated. "She never made it to Georgia. And not only do I have *her* confession, my overseer informed me that he had the… *pleasure* of speaking to you that night as well."

McLeary felt the blood escape his cheeks.

"If it should ease your mind some," the planter continued, "Betty will be free this time tomorrow because I don't have the patience to keep her around any longer."

"Why you gettin' angry wit' me if she gonna be free anyways?"

"Because it is the *principle* of it, sir!" Powell's voice thundered. "You tried to take *my* property away from me, and in doing so, you have wronged me in such a way that cannot be forgiven. Sir, you should be hanged! And you would be, too, if not for the fact that I intend to send you to the grave myself."

"Now, er, hold up a minute there." McLeary tried to keep his voice calm and steady. "Henry, I ain't freed Betty without good cause to do so."

"What do you mean?"

"I's angry wit' ye," he admitted, "'cause I heard ye 'n' Booth talkin' at the party. Y'all was sayin' how ye be wantin' to keep guns in my place for yer… fightin' or whutever's ye got brewin' wit' them boys from South Carolina. Ye be sayin' how I's takin' the blame if this plan o' y'alls gets figered out."

For a moment, it appeared that the planter would lower his gun. His eyes flickered, lost in his own thoughts. But the barrel stayed trained upon its target.

"I knew I never should have involved you in this." Powell shook his head. "There's a deal that the men and I made — I'll say this much — a promise that we will take action against the government if Lincoln wins in November. Yes, should the circumstances come to it, we will fight back if any northerner comes down here and thinks he can strip us of our rights. And yes, it's my job to convince you to be the man who will protect our supplies for us. But let me be very clear about this — I did *not* agree to have our operation be dependent almost entirely upon you. That's too much stake vested into one person. Rather, *I* was going to invite you to join our militia, and the degree of your involvement would've been up to you to decide.

To a degree, I share your frustration — admittedly so. I share your fears. These are uncertain times we are living in, and I *know* that the worst is yet to come. But you had an awful lot of gall to act upon your impulses in such a way that jeopardized my reputation. If word starts getting out that I've got runaways, no one will do business with me. McLeary, I thought you were a man of good character, but it appears that you're nothing more than a feeble-minded fool. Your actions, no matter how well-intentioned you think they were, deserve severe punishment, and so you shall bear it."

"Hold on, now, jest a minute longer."

"Your time's running out, McLeary…"

"Be this grudge o' yers so bitter that ye *really* be willin' to take my life? Ye don' want no blood on yer hands, do ya?"

"Don't consider it a grudge — think of it as retribution. Regardless, I'll sleep well at night knowing I've sent you to your grave; that much you can be assured of, sir."

"Wuh you gonna git from shootin' me? Some sorta ovation from yer buddies?"

"You can count on it."

"Why ye gotta be this way, Henry?"

"What way?"

"Thinkin' yer so high 'n' mighty cause ye got some hands to work the fields 'n' rake in the money for ya. I's willin' to bet ye ain't made a cent from yer own efforts."

"Dangerous words coming from a man who's about to taste lead."

"Dangerous how? Cause ye knows I be right?"

"This is coming from the man who I am to believe is *not* an abolitionist?"

"Don' know none 'bout abolition."

"Your actions that night suggested otherwise."

"Ye gotta problem 'cause I knows the difference between right 'n' wrong?"

"You've got some nerve…"

"Not as much nerve as you do, roundin' up slaves 'n' makin' them do yer biddin' like you's a king or somethin'."

"I'll have you know I treat my slaves with great care. You've seen it yourself, and don't try to deny it."

"Fine. I'll go on 'n' play along even though it ain't true. You could treat 'em real nice — feed 'em good 'n' get 'em this or that… But I don' see you wantin' to trade places wit' 'em."

"I wouldn't."

"That be exactly my point."

"Well, then, thank you for making it known. Here's my rebuttal…"

Powell raised the barrel and pulled the trigger. A deafening pop rang out. A puff of smoke obscured his vision, but it was only temporarily…

McLeary lay glassy-eyed and limp in a mangled heap on the grass, a fresh wound gaping in the center of his chest. The lantern lay broken at his side; shards of glass littered the ground. As quickly as it came, its orange glow was extinguished. The chill night air sent a shiver down Powell's spine. The deed was done, and there was no use dwelling upon it any further. There was a home to return to and a warm bed to sleep in. Not that there was much sleep to be had — not tonight anyway.

The planter turned and made his way towards his horses, which stood wide-eyed and trembling. He climbed into the carriage, tugged on the reins, and took one last look at his work. The corner of his lips raised to a smirk.

Good riddance.

Chapter 10

There was great commotion in the pub. Men laughed and hollered over one another, wrapped up in fits of merriment and leisure. It was another ordinary night at the Broken Mug. Shane Doyle sat propped at the far end of the bar, sipping away at a bottomless pint. He had lost count of his drinks, but at least he had had enough to get blood pumping and a good buzz going.

It had only been a few days since his business had been torched, and since that time he had made his way to the bar like a priest to mass. Indeed, it was habitual, almost cleansing, to lose himself in the drinks. To turn away from a reality that was far too daunting to confront. His business was quite literally in ruins, and any hope of salvaging what was left would have been in vain.

In a world that knew only grim happenstance and hard luck, there was one certainty that he could take comfort in — those responsible for his suffering would pay dearly. Doyle took a swill from his pint and scowled. Visions of Robert Hill toyed with his thoughts, in which he offered toasts to crowds of supporters to celebrate the defeat of a hated rival. The very thought of what Hill might have been up to made his blood boil. *Selfish bastard*, the Irishman fumed. *I'll give you what's yours soon enough.*

"Beg your pardon," a voice called over to him.

He was an older man, lean and trim, whose creased brow and sunken cheeks had been worn down by years of unyielding grit and determination. There was a fire in his eyes that captured a youthful spirit, rebellious and uncompromising. He wore a dark suit, finely pressed and fitted comfortably to his figure.. Although there was an air of prestige about him, it was clear enough that he was no ordinary elitist. He was a man who had ventured into the lions' den time and time again, and more than likely yearned for more.

"Mr Doyle?"

"I believe that's me, last time I checked…"

"I've been told I would find you here. You're a regular, I take it?"

"A regular? More like a resident…"

"Mind if I take a seat?"

"Seeing as I am a man among the masses," Doyle remarked, "you're more than welcome to take mine if you'd like."

"Well, actually," the gentleman said, chuckling, "that's not what I had in mind. I was hoping to speak with you."

"Me?" Doyle laughed and shook his head. "I didn't think my name meant much these days. Well, as long as you're not here to make a fool out of me, I suppose you can speak about whatever's on your mind."

"Rest assured, Mr Doyle," the stranger said as he nodded and hoisted himself onto a barstool, "there will be no mockery here. I'm a fan of yours. In fact, I'd like to think of us as allies…"

"Allies, eh?" The Irishman took another sip from his glass. "If that's the case, then we're fighting a losing battle."

"I'm aware of your situation," was the response, "and if I may say so, sir, this 'battle' you speak of is far from over. In fact, I want to help you pack a punch that will send a certain 'friend' of yours, shall we say, along with his accomplices, to the ground."

Doyle arched his brow and eyed the stranger closely. "Who are you?"

"My apologies, sir." The man extended his hand. "Name's Thaddeus Stevens. Representative of Pennsylvania's Ninth District."

"Representative? You're a congressman?"

"That's correct, sir."

Doyle cracked a smile and the two shook hands.

"Is a congressman's day so monotonous that he wastes it away by having meaningless conversations with men like me?"

"I wouldn't say that," Stevens replied. "In fact, men like you are sought after for your extraordinary commitment to the abolitionist cause. Speaking with you is a real treat."

"Well, if you are as informed about my situation as you say you are," Doyle said, shifting in his seat, "then you'll know it'll take more than a 'punch' to ensure that amends are made."

"I couldn't agree more." Stevens nodded. "Which is why you and I have something important to discuss. Mr. Doyle, have you heard anything about me?"

"With all due respect, sir," he answered, "for years the only voice I've heard is my own. I was the only one who stood up to injustice, and they burned me for it — no pun intended."

"Let me assure you, then, that you're not alone in the fight. The number of abolitionists is growing every day in this country, and word of your… *misfortune* has been made known to several colleagues of mine."

"Colleagues, eh? I'd appreciate it if you don't use my story as leverage in whatever game you're playing in Washington."

"This is no game, sir." Stevens shook his head. "Should you feel so inclined, we wish to provide you with the means to right certain wrongs, if you catch my drift…"

Doyle let out a hearty laugh and chugged down his beer. "I come off as that desperate, do I?" he spouted and slammed the pint on the counter. "You're a politician at heart, Mr Stevens, but the offer is welcomed nonetheless. How can you assist me?"

"Well, for starters," Stevens whispered and leaned in close. Slowly, carefully, he reached into his jacket and produced a small revolver. He bowed the handle towards the Irishman. "Consider this to be a donation from Uncle Sam."

***

He had to have been out of his mind. An utter madman, racing around the streets with nothing but a burning rage. Doyle had showed up at his front door, red-faced and grinning, ready to storm off to the races. The scent hit Streicher immediately. He must have had one too many drinks only moments prior, but that did not matter. The Irishman boasted that he would give Mr Hill 'a good beating,' and that Streicher was more than welcome to tag along to witness the occasion. Having endured several days' worth of chastisement from his father, particularly about how his work was better off wasting away as 'a useless pile of ash,' he was ready to unleash his fury. And no man, not even his father, deserved it more than Robert Hill.

The young man gladly accepted Doyle's invitation, and before long the two were parading down the city streets. Apparently, the Hill residence was hosting a special outing, undoubtedly to celebrate a corrupt victory. It was the perfect opportunity to strike back, and with any luck, Doyle would knock that sack of filth to the floor right in front of his friends. Of course, any scheme that Doyle had up his sleeve would not compare to the gross injustice that was done unto them. Not by a long shot. Still, it would be nice to watch that man get his keister handed to him again. And for all he knew, maybe Emma would take a peep to see it too…

Emma…

The very thought of her made his legs stiff and breath short. He had responded to her letter, offering weak sentiments and false encouragement. *All will be made well soon enough*, he wrote, and he assured her that *only sound judgements, choices of a good nature* would be made in the coming months. She was right, after all. There *was* a future to look after, and she would be most displeased if he ever acted in a way that jeopardized it.

You're too good for this world, Emma, he thought, sighing. *Far, far too good…*

A festering guilt quickly overcame him, but it was not enough to overpower his anger. She was likely unaware of the crime her father had committed, and therefore she could not possibly understand the depth of the conflict. How could any man not spring to action after such an injustice? Retaliation was not only justifiable — it was demanded.

Keep patient, he implored himself. *In a few months, you can say goodbye to all of this.*

The towering mansion basked in the orange glow of a setting sun. As they proceeded down the driveway, their strides becoming steady and quick, Streicher saw the beady-eyed mogul greeting guests with a stone face and solemn nods. The usual welcome. Behind him stood a small cluster of men, all dressed in fine attire, with arms folded and smirks fixed upon their faces.

"They must be his yes-men," Doyle muttered. "Stay behind me, lad. I'll do the talking…"

All heads turned in their direction as they ventured closer to the entrance. The parade of guests was gone, and only Streicher and the Irishman remained. At the sight of them, Hill's eyes lit up.

"Ah, *now* you're in for quite a treat, gentlemen," Hill commented and cocked his head towards his companions. "These are the two freedom fighters."

A string of snide remarks and snickers lingered in the air. Streicher stood several paces behind his former employer, who stormed over to Hill with hands on his hips.

"Funny," Doyle said, nodding. "Real funny. Glad to see that you've still got that wonderful sense of humor."

"Some things never change."

"I guess not."

Streicher cast his gaze towards a large window. In the great hall, guests exchanged laughter and radiant smiles, all dressed to the nines. Every member of the city's elite must have been in attendance. From corner to corner, he scanned the room and frowned. No sign of Emma.

"My apologies," said Hill, cracking a smirk and folding his arms, "but I believe neither of you were given an invitation."

"We don't want anything to do with your little 'outing,' or whatever this is," the Irishman snapped.

"So then, if I may inquire, to what do I owe the pleasure?"

Doyle reached into his pocket, eyes bulging and cheeks flushed, and produced the only piece of evidence from the crime — Hill's note. "You tell us, you worthless sack of shit!"

The men laughed and Hill calmly reached for the paper. "Such vulgar language, Mr. Doyle," he remarked. "I expected more from a man who prides himself on having such high morals. I thought you were supposed to be a humanitarian of sorts. An honest, good-natured abolitionist."

"Don't test me," the Irishman warned. "You know exactly why I'm here."

"Certainly." Hill nodded and handed the note back to him. "Show that to the court, if you'd like. State the truth for what it is — grovel and howl about it until you're blue in the face. But know that I am a force in this city. No court would convict me of any charges, even if I confessed. Let this be a lesson to you, Mr. Doyle: know your opponent before you go after them."

A raw silence lingered as Doyle stood frozen. Streicher's breath grew short — something was about to give. A good slug between the eyes was ideal...

182

"Under normal circumstances, I'd agree with you," Doyle said softly. "But there's a flaw with your theory."

"Do tell…"

"Being a man of such power," he went on, "you're suggesting that you have no limitations. No weaknesses. But I am here to tell you that you do."

"I'm listening…"

"Well, though you may be a great force, I'd wager that you're not capable of stopping a bullet."

Hill's eyes narrowed. "Is that a threat?"

"No." Doyle shook his head. "I'd like to think of it more as justice served."

It was a blur. Almost too quick to comprehend. Streicher watched, wide-eyed and breathless, as Doyle whipped out a revolver from his pocket and aimed it at his foe. Two pops. Hill collapsed upon the stone pavement. Men roared and scrambled about. An exchange of gunfire. Doyle landed hard upon the ground as a swarm of Hill's cohorts piled on top of him. The blood fled Streicher's cheeks. His heart raced as men sharpened their gazes upon him, their faces contorted in fits of wild rage. He longed to free himself from his spell, but his legs refused to move. As quick as a flash of lightning, he was thrown from his balance and sent to the stone floor. Hands restrained him and frantically searched his pockets. Panicked voices echoed above him.

"Is he armed?"

"Take whatever you can find!"

"Don't let him up!"

Streicher raised his head slightly. He strained his eyes to see a large crowd gathered beside Hill, who lay sprawled upon the ground with his eyes closed, unmoving.

Perhaps there should have been remorse. Instant regret. But a smirk came to his lips instead.

Good riddance.

PART II

Chapter 11

Richmond, Virginia
November 6, 1860

The air was heavy and raw. Bright rays poured through wisps of clouds, marking the start of a day that came with both promise and dread. Men arrived in droves to the courthouses and stood in lines that had no end. Some chatted excitedly to one another about the uncertainties of the day, offering their own thoughts and theories about its outcome; others waited in silent anticipation. It seemed that all voters had their decisions made, convictions firm, but that did not stop Henry Powell from pestering them as they waited to cast their ballots.

"Come now, boys! Come now!" He clapped his hands as he made his way down the line, eyeing voters as he strolled past. "Preserve our interests and our way of life — vote for John Bell! Hear me again and hear me well — vote for John Bell!"

"Bell for president!" a voice hollered out.

"I stand with Breckenridge!" another declared.

"We need a moderate choice," a third chimed in. "Stephen Douglas for president!"

Voices escalated and before long a spirited shouting match broke out.

"Settle down, gentlemen!" Powell hollered above the ruckus, laughing. "Settle down! Can't we all agree that we'd rather have anyone but Lincoln?"

His remark was met with howls of laughter, thunderous applause, and choruses of "Hear! Hear!" A toothy grin came to his lips. Yet another rousing ovation from the public gallery. The planter chuckled to himself, reached into his pocket, and lit up a cigar. It had been the right decision to travel to Richmond. Why waste the day away at Shady Grove when there were was a much larger audience to entertain at the capital?

He had cast his ballot at the crack of dawn, which meant that the rest of the day could be spent riling up crowds of voters. Of course, a few drinks and cigars would be had as well. It was a day of celebration. Of promise. His high spirits did not seem to be shared among the masses, at least from what he could tell, but that mattered little to him. Very few matched his keen intelligence, which meant that they were unable to foresee that Lincoln was destined to be defeated. He simply did not have enough support to carry the swing states, and he most certainly would not win over the support of southerners. As far as the other candidates were concerned, it was admittedly a toss-up. But no matter who won, they all vowed to protect southern rights, and therefore his business would be safe.

This time tomorrow, you will remain the top of the heap once again, Powell mused to himself as he puffed away.

"Causing more trouble, I take it?" A voice spoke from behind him.

The planter spun around to find Booth facing him, arms folded.

"Ah, there is the debonair himself!" Powell extended his hand and they shook. "How are you, John?"

"About as well as any sane man can be," he remarked flatly, "when the day of reckoning is upon us."

"Day of reckoning?" The planter laughed. "I think those dramatics have gotten into your head, boy!"

"I wish I could share your optimism."

"I wish you could too." Powell gnawed away at his cigar. "I wish a lot of people could."

"How did I know you would wind up here?"

"Guess you know me too well."

"Either that," Booth countered, "or you're too predictable."

"Perhaps." Powell nodded. "I'm not one who keeps many people guessing…"

"It's good to know there's at least some certainty left in this world."

"Oh, lighten up, John! The world's not coming down on us, now, is it?"

"No," was the response. "Not yet, anyway."

"Lincoln's not going to win."

"Keep telling yourself that."

"I will." Powell stuck his cigar in between his lips and smiled. "And I'll sleep well tonight."

"You don't have many restless nights, do you?"

"Not recently."

"How are things at the plantation?" Booth asked. "I hope for your sake that your little Fourth of July 'incident' has been resolved."

"Indeed, it has."

"You found your nigger?"

"I did."

"Good." Booth nodded. "She wasn't too bright running off on you like that."

"No," the planter agreed, "but she wasn't without help."

"Help?" The young actor arched his brow. "It was coordinated?"

Powell nodded slowly. He lowered his voice and said, "By none other than our dear friend Thomas McLeary."

"McLeary?" Booth gasped. "That bastard! I knew there was something about him…"

"Fooled me plain enough."

"Did you…"

Powell made a gun with his hand and pretended to fire.

"And he's…"

The planter nodded.

"My God…" he muttered, his face ashen. "How is Mrs. McLeary handling all of this?"

"She doesn't know the wiser," Powell said solemnly, "and as far as I'm concerned, that's how it ought to be."

"What does she think happened to him?"

"That he ran off," was the response. "That's what I told her, anyway. She came to the market the next day, all dressed in black, crying and moaning and making all sorts of a fuss. Can't say that I blame her though — it's not *her* fault her husband was such a back-stabbing scoundrel. 'Thomas has gone missing,' she cried out to me. 'We went to bed last night, and when I woke up this morning, he was gone!' I told her to keep calm and remain patient. I assured her that I would scour the countryside night and day to find her 'dear' husband. It was an answer that she seemed to be content with for the time being, and that was good enough for me. Gave it a few days more, and then I came to her door — hat off, real somber, you know — see, John? I can be an actor too! — and I said, 'I'm terribly sorry, Alice. I've looked all around this blessed town and beyond and there's no sign of your husband. For as much as it pains me to say this, it appears that he may have run off on you.' Well, next thing I know she starts wailing and hollering unlike anything my ears have ever heard. I gave her my shoulder and then she starts screaming at the sky, using words that I never knew were in a Richmond girl's vocabulary. Sure, I do have sympathy

191

for the poor woman — she's always been upstanding and courteous. Certainly didn't deserve the fate she was given. But her husband, the scheming rat that he was, *did* deserve his. And for that I will not apologize. Not to anyone."

"Nor should you," Booth agreed. "What's Mrs. McLeary up to these days?"

"Hardly anything, I reckon," the planter stated. "Stays cooped up in her house all day, but that's not much of a change from her previous life. She's sociable enough — you've met her yourself — but I think McLeary kept her locked away so he could have her to himself."

"What do you mean?"

"She's..." Powell's voice faltered. "She's a remarkable woman — quite the socialite, as I said. It's a conundrum how she ended up with a man like McLeary. Alice has always been a free spirit, for as long as I've known her. I remember the days when we were younger and her father would take her to Shady Grove. She caught the attention of all the young men in town, myself included. What a pity it was that she married a hermit — that sort of lifestyle never suited her. She would have been better off among her own kind, hobnobbing with the rest of Richmond's elite." The planter offered a weak smile.

"No sense in dwelling on what might have been," Booth replied.

"I suppose not."

"Sooner or later, reality will catch up to *all* of us, much as it did to Mrs. McLeary."

"Don't play that game with me, John," Powell warned. "I don't appreciate your pessimism…"

"Fine," he retorted, "but don't come crying to me when Lincoln sends troops to turn that haven of yours into a pile of rubble."

"*You're* the one who needs to find some sense," the planter remarked angrily. "I'll admit, John, I'm not fond of the man myself — he's as looney as they come… but you're making him out to be the devil incarnate."

"That's because he is. And quite honestly, it's baffling how *you* of all people aren't able to see it."

"Watch your mouth, son."

"You know I'm right."

"And what exactly do you expect me to do if the man wins? Sure, I'll fight — but I won't single-handedly win the war."

"You say you'll fight, but I'm not convinced…"

"I've fought in battle, alright? Don't tell me what I will or won't do…"

"But you've never fought a battle like *this* before. Not against your own countrymen."

"Neither have you."

"But I will. Gladly."

"Sure." Powell chuckled. "And when the day comes when you trade in your playbills for a gun, let me know."

"If Lincoln has his way, you can bet on it…"

"I look forward to it," the planter said sarcastically.

"You won't be the only one…"

"Well, John," Powell let out a long drag and watched the black smoke dissipate, "I regret to inform you that I can take only so much of this sort of talk. If you're willing to let that head of yours come down some, I welcome you to join me and some of the boys tonight for a few celebratory drinks."

"I'll partake," Booth reluctantly replied, "but do yourself a favor and let loose *before* you get to the bar. You won't want to remember this day…"

"Until tonight, John."

As the actor disappeared into the bustling crowds, Powell shook his head in disgust. No one would dampen his spirits. Not tonight, when there was so much to take joy in, so much to be thankful for…

Lincoln was bound to lose. He did not have a chance, not with his rhetoric…

Keep telling yourself that, Henry.

The planter sighed as he threw his cigar to the ground and squashed it with his boot. It was time for a drink.

***

He prayed that his drink would provide some remedy for his diminished spirits. A distant hope, it most certainly was, but it was better than having no hope at all. As the day neared its end, he had had too many to count. But all that he was left with was the same longing he had when he first took his seat.

Powell sat at a crowded table among friends whose faces grew increasingly blurred and their names more difficult to pronounce. Under normal circumstances, he would have indulged in the companionship, but what the night brought with it was anything but ordinary. Booth lay sprawled in the seat next to him, glassy-eyed and glistening with sweat, and he took swills from a pint like it was his job. Unfavorable results, which seemed more and more frequent with every hour, were met with "Damn it!" and the slam of a fist upon a tabletop. When the news was good, the actor led the bar in a spirited "Hallelujah!"

Results were flooding rapidly into Washington. Most were predictable enough: Lincoln dominated New England and northwestern states like Michigan and Illinois; the Deep South belonged to Breckenridge. As was to be expected, the country's fate belonged to the middle-ground states of Ohio, Indiana, and Pennsylvania.

Once lively and rambunctious, the place was overcome by a lingering silence. Lincoln or Breckenridge would win the day… and all had a hunch as to who it would be. A sense of dread prevailed in the crowded room. The inevitable was quickly approaching…

Then more results came in.

Tennessee — Winner: Bell.

Kentucky — Winner: Bell.

Virginia — Winner: Bell.

He should have been relieved. Elated. Thanking his lucky stars. His candidate was putting up a respectable fight. But the dread only persisted. It was a losing fight. Powell sighed as his head collapsed into his hands. A fractured southern alliance would prove fatal, he feared. Without a united front, there would not be enough momentum for Breckenridge to capture much-needed electoral votes. Unless by some miracle…

Palms clammy and brow coated with sweat, Powell reached into his pocket, pulled out a handkerchief, and dabbed himself. There was only so much more that he could take.

Then the southern cause, so passionately cherished and defended by its proponents, was shattered entirely.

Ohio — Winner: Lincoln.

Indiana — Winner: Lincoln.

Pennsylvania — Winner: Lincoln.

In a moment of clarity, the world around him came alive. For the first time all night, he heard his friends' cries of rage and anguish. He saw their tear-filled eyes and reddened faces. There was a rawness in the air, which left his lips dry and parched. All around him, emotions ran high… and yet he was numb. He sat stone-faced with his hand cupped around his drink, seeing everything and feeling nothing. Perhaps there should have been some crack of a whip. Some jolt that would have sent him leaping to his feet, just as it had done to

Booth, who hurled his pint clear across the room and stormed out in a silent rage.

But as the patrons raced about with frenzy and outrage, the planter remained where he sat. Nothing else mattered. Not tonight. He would finish his drink and retire for the night to his hotel room. It would be a soundless sleep, and in the morning, the day would be new.

No need to fret, Henry, he assured himself. *All will soon be made well again. One way or another. All will be made well again…*

Chapter 12

The air was light and refreshing. A calm breeze made its way through the rolling plains: a much-needed comfort in a broken world. Emma Hill sat with her hands folded in her lap, gazing upon the sprawling landscape. The sky was cloudless and bright, and as the sun's rays warmed her cheeks, she closed her eyes and embraced the comfort of a pleasant autumn day.

More and more, she found herself closing her eyes in solitude, praying that when they were reopened, the past would right itself and her world would be in order again. But after four months, no miracle was to be found. Her eyes opened to a reality that filled her with dread and despair. No sunny skies or cheery clouds could erase what had happened…

She let out a long sigh.

Erich…

The name flooded her thoughts every second of the day. He was a cherished memory that lived on only in her heart. Not so long ago, she had been able to take comfort in his arms and drift away into the joy of every moment. He had always been there for her, providing a shoulder to lean on, offering words of support and encouragement — he had been the perfect gentleman.

A tear streamed Emma's cheek.

She should have done more...

She had begged the courts to spare his life. He was an innocent man, she had declared too many times to count. There was no weapon found upon him; only Doyle was guilty of that charge. If there was anyone who deserved to be punished for her father's death, it was the Irishman. But despite her efforts and the power that came with her name, her father's reputation was stronger. No man who was a suspect could wipe his hands of the mess. After two months of expedited hearings when, coincidentally, more and more 'evidence' was uncovered about Streicher's participation (in one instance, a letter that had been fraudulently written in his name — undoubtedly penned by one of Hill's associates — stated his intentions to carry out the murder with Doyle), the two men had found themselves condemned to the noose.

She had never been permitted to visit her love behind bars. Not even a passing glance was acceptable. Streicher's final day, much to her grief and dismay, was spent without her. Often she dreamed of what their future would have been like if the nightmare never happened, but it only brought her great pain. Tears flowed steadily down her cheeks.

Only an arm's reach away sat a diary on a small, circular table. The only solace she took in a shattered world was written in those pages. There was something strangely satisfying about writing down her own thoughts, even if she dreaded confronting them. With her pen, she could say whatever she wanted — there were no rules or restrictions. She was the crafter of every word, thought, and phrase. The pages were hers to control. With a deep breath, she reached forward and grabbed her pen and diary, flipped to a blank page, and began to write:

November 1860

Wednesday, 14th. The sun lights up the sky with a bright blaze and casts its warmth upon all living creatures below. It must be that I am immune to its natural charm, for my spirit is weak and beaten. I do not feel its warmth. I feel hardly anything at all. It is clear that God has cast His shadow over me — am I ever to be happy again?

Despite his kind hospitality, this stay at Uncle Joseph's place has done little to liven my mood. I am lost — trapped. Remaining here only serves to confirm my fears, a dreaded reality that came storming down upon me months ago. The past was real, and it can never be changed. Going back to Philadelphia would only make matters worse, and I dare not dream of what is to become of me if I have to confront horrid memories back at the old house. It is as if I am on a ship with no sails. Without course or direction.

But it would be selfish to dwell upon my own circumstances any further, for I fear that there is a much bigger storm coming. There is much talk about secession in this state, and the threat of armed resistance seems more and more real since Mr. Lincoln's victory. Uncle Joseph speaks of it with a growing enthusiasm, but I cannot help but be overcome with dread by the talk of it. I would die a thousand deaths if it meant sparing others the grief that has consumed me.

Slavery is an inherent evil in this country because of its cruel, divisive nature. It seems that even rational heads cannot agree one way or another on the subject, and I fear the course that we are heading will lead to great suffering on both sides. This country must tread carefully, or there will be many who will suffer tragedies as I have.

"There you are, Emma! I thought you'd run off on me!"

Emma jumped. With a quick turn of her head, she glanced up and saw her cousin, Grace Adams, who cast her a wide grin. Always smiling and ever-enthused, Grace possessed stunning brown eyes that flashed with the same excitement and wonder as a child on Christmas morning. She kept her shining dark hair fastened into a bun and wore a light green sundress that flowed gently in the breeze.

The two young ladies had never seen each other as much as they had in the past two months, and Grace took great joy in having a companion at the plantation. Although her company was pleasant enough, Emma often preferred to be left alone. But it seemed that whenever there was a chance to escape into her thoughts, that same voice (which, admittedly, was becoming a bit of a nuisance) interrupted her.

"Forgive me, cousin," Grace said, chuckling, "I didn't mean to frighten you."

"Don't apologize," Emma murmured as she closed her notebook.

"Mind if I join you?" her cousin asked and propped herself in the seat beside her.

I suppose I don't have much of a choice, Emma thought, careful not to roll her eyes.

"Lost again in that fantasy world of yours, are you?"

"If that's how you want to put it…"

"Only joking." Grace laughed and swatted playfully at her wrist. "Come on, Emma, give me a smile."

"Not today, I'm afraid."

"What's wrong?"

"Nothing."

"You can tell me, Emma. Please."

"Don't worry about it."

"Emma…"

"What do you expect me to say?"

"What I *expect*," her cousin's tone became firm, "is for you to be honest with me. You've looked absolutely miserable since you've arrived here, and it doesn't do you any good keeping all those thoughts of yours tucked away. Now, let's try this again — what's wrong?"

"Quite frankly, Grace," Emma said, sighing, "I think you know the answer already."

Silence.

"Yes, I reckon I do," she admitted. "But — I mean this in the nicest way — there comes a time when you must look towards the future. There's no use in carrying on as you have. I doubt both your father and Erich would want you to wallow in misery."

"Move on, is that what you're saying?"

"Well, in a way, yes."

"That's easy for you to say…"

"Please, Emma," her cousin implored her, "don't take any offense. I only think that it'd be in your best interest to live life again. Get out of the house for a bit — maybe go to the theatre or some of the local shops. It may help to brighten your spirits."

"It won't."

Silence.

That was enough of that, at least for one day…

"There's been a buzz in town recently." Grace spoke slowly. "Apparently the state legislature is quite adamant that Mr. Lincoln poses a threat to southern interests. A resolution was passed to declare South Carolina's intention to secede from the Union."

All Emma could do was shake her head…

"Personally, I believe they are in their right to do so," Grace continued, then added with a smirk, "but I guess I shouldn't let my tongue run too much in the presence of a northerner."

"Do you want war, Grace?"

"Well, I don't wish for it," she answered, "but if that's what it takes for this country to settle its differences, then I suppose there's no other alternative."

"What's it like in town?"

"What do you mean?"

"The men — do they want war?"

"You should see for yourself." Grace laughed. "Many of the men — boys too — are arriving in droves to sign up to join the militia. Many are bringing their guns. They keep on cheering and boasting about how they're going to whoop some federal troops. It really is a sight to see!"

"I'm sure it is."

"If it's war that you're concerned about," was the response, "I wouldn't fret too much. There will likely be a few fists exchanged, but all in sport. Like gentlemen do, you understand. Nothing more."

"Since when was war considered to be 'sport'?"

"Really, Emma, I think you're blowing this a bit out of proportion, if I may say so."

"And I think you're being foolish… if I may say so."

"I beg your pardon?"

"When it's *your* father who is killed by a bullet," Emma's voice shook, "or a bayonet, or succumbs to some other horrific fate altogether, you'll know what I mean."

"My goodness, Emma, you really shouldn't say such things."

"It doesn't matter what I say. If war is to come, then there's no avoiding it. But I'd caution anyone who's overly optimistic about its outcome."

"I think that head of yours has gotten you into quite a rut." Grace eyed her with concern. "It can be easy to feel like the world's against you, especially with the year you've had. But don't lose hope. Sooner or later, all will be made well again. Now, if you'll excuse me…" She stood, flattened the wrinkles in her dress, and said, "I have a supper to prepare."

As her footsteps grew faint, Emma sighed and rolled her eyes. *Sure, Grace, I'll play along.* She shook her head. *All will be made well again…*

Chapter 13

Powell craved the attention. Wondering faces surrounded him, eager to hear his wisdom and perspective on the matters of the day. From the mouths of friends and strangers alike, the questions came pouring down upon him.

"Do you really think South Carolina will secede, Henry?"

"What's to become of Virginia?"

"How should we prepare ourselves if the federals come down here to meet us?"

"Will you lead the charge for us?"

It was another early morning at the town market, bustling and frantic. Always the debonair, Powell smiled, calmly held up a hand, and lit a cigar.

"Easy does it, gentlemen." He chuckled. "Let's not get ourselves in a fit by worrying about the uncertainties of the future."

Again, he was met with questions.

"But what about Lincoln? Don't you suppose he'll send all of Washington upon us if there's a rebellion?"

"Do we have enough guns to mount a resistance? What about food and supplies?"

"How should we protect our families?"

The planter raised the cigar to his lips and shoved a hand into his pocket.

"Keep up the chirping," he teased, "and I'll put all of you to work with my slaves."

Laughter erupted around him.

"In all seriousness," the planter went on, "I do share some of your concerns. But I can't — nor *will* I — lose sleep on thoughts and theories that are grounded in fiction. All this talk about fighting has no more basis of fact than saying the sun rises in the west and sets in the east.

Gentlemen, I have seen war with my own eyes, and it is an ugly thing, plain and simple. I do not want violence; God forbid it ever comes to our front doors. Rest assured though, I will be there with each and every one of you to protect what is rightfully ours, should the circumstances come to it. But to get ourselves in a frenzy over speculation is plain absurd and irresponsible. If the day should come when we must have a conversation about such matters, let it happen in time. For now, though, I suggest we remain content and go about business as usual."

His reception was mixed. There were a few nods, several head shakes, and a chorus of impassioned banter. It did not matter what he said one way or another. Emotions ran high and convictions were unbreakable; he could only do his best to try to avoid setting anyone into a panic.

Although calm and collected in public, his demeanor was much different behind closed doors. In the weeks following the election, he had spent too much time pacing about the halls in his mansion, bogged down by his own fears, frustrations, and wild thoughts. Lincoln's victory posed a direct threat to his business and livelihood, and there was nothing to stop the entire U.S. Army from surrounding his property with cannons and loaded rifles.

His blood boiled at the very notion of abolition, but the movement had nonetheless become more vocal over the past month. Who were they to denounce his business as cruel and unjust? Who were they to smear his character in such a way that supported their myth of the southern planter?

He had been called evil.

He had been called vile.

And he had had enough.

No soldier would set foot on his property without being met by a blaze of gunfire. Since the death of McLeary, his entire outlook on civil conflict had changed. He could kill his fellow countrymen and not blink an eye, so long as they were the aggressor. And the aggressor, 'they' — be it abolitionists, Lincoln, or free states — most certainly were.

He had not done anything wrong. His business was perfectly legal, and so long as it was protected by the Constitution, he had every right to live as he chose. Many nights were spent lying awake, overcome by anger and frustration. If there was war to come, by God, he would fight…

An unusual sight stirred him from his thoughts. Beyond the crowd, dressed in all black, was a small figure. A woman. Powell strained his eyes as he studied her approaching the group. Age must have taken its toll on her, for she hobbled towards the market with slow, careful steps. His breath grew short as her features became clearer in the emerging daylight. It was time to return home.

"Forgive me, gents." Powell bowed his head. "I best be on my way — lots of business to attend to."

As he slipped through the crowd, careful to remain hidden, he made his way quickly towards his carriage. But not before a soft voice, coarse and weak, beckoned to him… "Won't you stay a little while longer, Henry?"

The planter spun around and met the weary gaze of Alice McLeary. With bloodshot eyes and a grey complexion, it appeared that she had aged ten years in four months. Her shining grey hair was tangled and unkempt; her clothes, wrinkled and caked with dirt and dust. For a moment, he feared that she would fall dead in front of him.

"Why, good morning, Alice." Powell mustered up a cheerful voice. "It's been too long, hasn't it? You're looking splendid…"

"Don't lie to me." She shook her head. "I look terrible, don't I?"

"To be frank with you, dear," he confessed, "you look ill. What brought you out of your home on a day such as this? Are you not feeling well?"

"You could say that," she wheezed out through heavy breaths, "but my affliction has not been brought upon by any disease. A broken heart, I fear, is what's done it to me."

"Still in mourning, are you?" said Powell, gently. "Truly, Alice, I am very sorry. If there's anything I can do, please say the word."

"What's done is done. Nothing can bring him back."

"I wish it wasn't so, my dear."

"They found him, you know."

"Pardon?"

"They found him dead in the woods," the old woman went on, "a week or so after he had gone missing. Somebody shot him, if you can believe it."

Powell froze, unable to think. Their conversation needed to end. Fast. "My, what a terrible tragedy that is," the planter remarked, desperately holding back the tremor in his voice. "Your husband was a good man; he didn't deserve such a fate."

"That's what I keep telling myself." Alice spoke softly. "After months and months of wrestling with my thoughts, it seems all I can do is ask why. Why Thomas, of all people? He was a good, honest man — you know this yourself. He never had a grudge with anybody."

"It truly is baffling how these misfortunes come about," Powell said. "Sometimes it makes one question their worth in the world."

"Indeed, it does," she concurred, nodding. "Well, in any case, I've found myself well enough to come here. Perhaps I am searching for answers in vain, but I wouldn't think highly of myself if I didn't try... Henry, do you know of anyone who had a quarrel with my husband?"

"Can't say that I do," the planter answered, slightly taken aback by his lie. There was a strange pleasure to it, knowing that the truth would be buried with him forever.

"I figured not."

"Your husband was a gentleman," Powell continued, "respected by many — and not to mention the master of his craft, as I liked to say. In all likelihood, he was a victim of tragic circumstance. He must have accidentally stumbled upon some bad company."

"I guess so," Alice murmured as her eyes sank to the ground, lost in sorrow.

"Believe me, Alice," he said, putting an arm around her shoulders, "if I had answers, I would have given them to you long before now. How about I give you a ride back to your place, alright? It may do you some good to rest for a while…"

With a gentle hand, he guided the grieving widow to his carriage and took control of the reins. His next move was clear: he needed to leave Shady Grove.

***

There was no time for surprises, yet the night's happenings had other plans for him. He was supposed to be on the road by now, marking the start of a three-month 'business venture' to collect new hands to help cultivate the fields (or, at least, that was the excuse he came up with). But instead, he found himself in the parlor, sharing drinks among his three companions — Brennan, Collett, and Knouse — who had arrived unexpectedly at his doorstep.

They had been on a week-long 'escapade' of their own, as they put it, to Richmond, and they thought it fitting to conclude their visit by spending the evening at the great mansion. Each of them brought along large wooden chests, which they placed by their feet. When Powell inquired about what was inside them, his friends exchanged glances with each other.

"Certain essential materials," Brennan said with a grin, "that would otherwise be of grave concern to many of our northern brethren, if they ever came upon them."

"For crying out loud, George, speak the King's English. What have y'all got in there?"

"Take a look for yourself…"

Brennan placed his chest upon the tabletop and threw the lid open: grey coats, neatly folded and finely decorated with golden buttons that ran up to the collar.

"It wouldn't be complete without the proper accessories," Collett added.

His box unveiled a load of canteens, which matched the color of the jackets. Belts sat in coils along the bottom, and Powell held one of them in his hands and studied the engraving upon the buckle.

"C.S.," he read and raised a brow at his friends. "What in heaven's name have you boys got up your sleeves?"

"It stands for Confederate States," Brennan explained, the smile still stuck to his face. "Well, more precisely, Confederate States of America."

"Confederate States of America?"

"That's right."

"What's it supposed to be — the ugly step-sister of the U.S.?"

"Think of it more as the favorite child. Everything that the U.S. is *supposed* to stand for — states' rights and personal liberties, while having a hands-off, don't-even-think-about-it approach towards federal intervention."

"And who was the grand architect behind this disaster?"

Knouse spoke up. "How do you know it'll be a disaster? And for the record, there were many of us behind this idea. A soon-to-be reality, as a matter of fact."

"We can't speak for any of the other states," Brennan began, "but South Carolina is serious about her intentions to secede, so much so that she will be the first state to be admitted to the Confederacy."

"It's plain theatrics, is what this is," Powell said, chuckling. "For as much as I admire the convictions of your home state, I doubt she'll last long once the Army of the Potomac gets word of this 'rebellion'."

"Don't be so sure," Collett remarked. "We've brought along more than clothes, if you catch my drift."

"Where on earth did you acquire these materials, gentlemen?"

"Several of Richmond's finest," Brennan said, jumping in, "agreed to aid our cause. I reckon there will be many more who will join in on the effort once the fighting commences."

"Certainly," Powell answered dryly, "and when Lincoln so much as hears of a whisper of trouble, he'll put everything to an end."

"What's gotten into you, Henry?" Knouse asked. "Don't you want to defend what's yours?"

"I do," he nodded, "and I will. But as the days go on, the more I fear that such efforts will be in vain."

"Have a little faith, my friend," Brennan implored him. "What's gotten you into such a foul mood?"

"I've had a spell of bad luck recently," was the answer. "I'm in need of a vacation."

"You're more than welcome to join us, if you'd like," Brennan offered. "You can stay at my plantation for as long as you need to."

"Thank you kindly, George," he said. "That would be swell. I'll take you up on your offer."

They polished off their drinks, and after Powell gave his wife a departing kiss, they made their way out to the front of the property. In the darkness, Powell made out three wagons, all loaded to the brim with chests, crates, and boxes.

"Does it bring back memories of the Indian Wars?" Brennan laughed and slapped him on the back. "If you don't mind, it'd be best if we travel through the night. No sense in attracting unwanted attention…"

The planter agreed, and he boarded the first wagon. It was time to move out.

***

The sky was stained black, except for the dull glow of the moon. All around them, towering trees and thick brush stood firm, as if to cloak them during their secret voyage. Only a soft rustle was heard every now and again in bushes, or the whisper of the wind as it scurried through branches. The three wagons made their way down a downtrodden dirt path, a sight so pitiful that it could very well have been neglected for decades.

Brennan took control of the reins of the first wagon with Powell seated beside him. Collett commanded the middle, and Knouse took up the rear. Their procession was slow and careful, a habit that only kept Powell's heart racing. As they ventured forth through the woods, his ears began to play tricks on him, and he repeatedly casted sharp glances towards the most minor disturbances.

Settle down, Henry, he pleaded to himself. *Just settle down…*

He needed to be patient, but time was not a luxury. If anything, they needed to move *faster* during the night hours to cover as much ground as possible. The thought of Charleston's tranquil waters and sunny skies toyed with him; he only wanted to put the past behind him… at least for the time being. Long enough to guarantee that any parties who were so inclined to investigate Thomas McLeary's sudden demise would have given up on their efforts prior to his return.

The wagons jostled and jolted at every bump in the road. Powell cast a glance behind him and peered through the white canvas: wooden boxes of all sizes stood clustered together in a complex puzzle. Such a feat must have been enough to impress any passerby. Whether or not they would approve of the contents was a different story…

"Exactly how much do you have in here, George?" the planter asked.

"Enough to start a war," Brennan said with a smile.

"Start a war, you say?" Powell said, chuckling nervously. "I'd wager you could very well *end* it too."

They journeyed on for what felt like too long, but eventually Powell's nerves began to ease. For a moment or two, he may have even dozed off. But the feeling of comfort — though it was certainly welcomed — fled as quickly as it came. In the distance, the valley sloped down below them. Dense woods opened to a clearing, and as the path meandered down the sprawling hillside, it led directly to a wooden bridge that sat above a small creek. Bathed in moonlight, draped in dark blue, a guard stood firmly at the entrance. A rifle was fixed to his side. Only a stone's throw away from his position was a small garrison, no bigger than a shack, that sat humbly under a waving federal flag.

"Patrol up ahead," Brennan called behind to the others. "Keep quiet and follow my lead. I'll see us on our way."

Are you mad? Powell thought helplessly. *This will be the end of us...*

Instinctively, he reached for his revolver, but as he rested his grip upon the handle, he recoiled. It was best to let the situation resolve itself. Besides, Brennan had the charm and know-how to smooth-talk his way out of a tight spot.

They approached the bridge casually, without any apparent urgency or haste. The guard studied them like a hawk. Unmoving, unflinching, he awaited their approach. It was only when the caravan lurched to a stop that he snatched his rifle in both hands and raised it ever so slightly. Though speedy and decisive, the gesture was

217

benign. Standard protocol, or so it seemed. But it was enough to make them understand that any sign of trouble would be met with a swift end…

With a furrowed brow and eyes that lit up like the moon, the soldier asked, "Where are you off to, gentlemen?"

"Just down the road-a-ways," Brennan said, smiling politely. "We want to make it to Cypher's Mill to rest for the night."

"Have you traveled long?"

"Too long to keep track, I'm afraid."

"Where are you coming from?"

"Washington."

"You've made it this far in one night?"

"Well, no — forgive me, sir — I thought you were inquiring about the origin of our travels. More recently, we've made our way here from Shady Grove."

"I see." The guard nodded slowly and eyed the wagon. "That's a respectable load you're carrying with you."

"It is," Brennan laughed. "I must say I agree with you."

"Might I inquire about the contents?"

"Only clothes and shoes."

"Clothes and shoes?"

"Yes, sir."

"Where are you taking them?"

"Charleston."

"For what purpose?"

"Slave auction."

"Slave auction?"

"That's right, sir."

The soldier nodded again, deep in thought. "Must be a respectable lot you're looking to sell," he remarked.

"It is, sir."

"How many? Roughly?"

"About one hundred... this time around, anyway."

"This errand you're running — is it on your behalf or someone else's?"

"Pardon?"

"Who's running the auction?"

"That would be me, sir."

"Name?"

"George Brennan."

"And the name of your business?"

"Brennan..." his voice faltered slightly, "...and Powell."

"Brennan and Powell?"

"Yes."

"The gentleman seated beside you is Powell, I assume?"

"Correct, sir."

"One last question..."

"Yes, sir?"

"What brings you out at such a time as this?"

"Necessity," Brennan's smile resurfaced, but it was strained. "We're out to make a profit, and quite honestly, the sooner we can get back, the sooner we can resume business. We tend to prefer traveling during the night hours as there is not as much traffic, as strange as it sounds."

"That's not strange at all," the soldier stated. "What *I* find strange is that there's not a single factory in Charleston that can provide you with clothes and shoes for your slaves. Why is that?"

Silence.

Powell spoke up. "A friend of ours in Washington cuts us a deal that's far better than any price in Charleston. It's worth the trip to save on costs, you understand."

"Can't say that I do…"

Flashes of movement caught Powell's attention. He cast a glance towards the garrison, where two armed soldiers filed out and eyed them intently.

At the sight of them, Brennan's eyes grew wide and his voice trembled slightly as he said, "We don't want any trouble."

"Neither do we," the guard responded, "but given the latest rumors of secesh in this country, certain precautions need to be taken."

"Of course, sir."

"Would you mind opening up one or two of your boxes for us?"

"Well, er, certainly."

Time stood still. There was a sudden rawness in the air, which left Powell stiff and rigid. The only sounds he heard were the thump of his companion's boots as they hit the ground and the crunch of each step he took as he sauntered to the rear of the wagon. Stone-faced and even-keeled, the guard shifted from his position and proceeded to meet Brennan, but he paused briefly and raised his gaze to Powell.

"Would you mind joining us too, sir?"

Ever so slightly, the planter slipped his hand into his pocket and tightened his grip upon the revolver.

"As you wish…"

"Gentlemen," he called out to Collett and Knouse, "I'd like you both to meet us as well…"

The four of them stood as if they were in a lion's den, surrounded by blue-clad uniforms and loaded guns. With prying eyes, the soldiers peered past them to take a closer look at their supply. Brennan stood before the massive assortment, his cheeks deeply pale and sickly. At his side, steadfast and focused, the guard gestured for him to proceed.

Brennan's arms shook frantically as he reached for the first box, a sight that made Powell's breath escape him. Collett and Knouse stood frozen, their faces as white as the moonlight. With a heavy sigh, the lid was pried open and they cast their sights upon a collection of grey coats.

"Open another one for me."

Brennan began to reach for a box next to it, but then paused. He reached for a different one…

"What's wrong with that one?"

"I'm sorry, sir?"

"The one beside you — you were going to open it up."

"Well, I…"

"What's in it?"

Silence.

Without a moment's hesitation, the guard shoved Brennan aside and feverishly ripped away the lid: guns. He tore off another one: ammunition. As Powell eased his finger on the trigger, an icy voice pierced the air.

"Gentlemen," the guard growled, "all this talk of secesh has gone too far for my liking. And it ends *now…*"

Ready to unleash destruction, he hastily raised the barrel of his rifle and aimed it in Brennan's direction. A shot rang out. The sickly-sweet scent of gunpowder flooded Powell's nostrils as he stood clutching his revolver in a trembling hand. When the smoke cleared, Brennan remained where he stood, arms raised, and the guard lay dead at his feet.

Instinct took control.

The sights of his revolver adjusted quickly, and he pointed his weapon towards the two remaining soldiers, who were scrambling to meet him with their guns. Powell took aim at the first and fired. A guttural cry pierced the sky as he collapsed upon the ground. Then came time for the second…

Knouse lunged at the soldier and desperately tried to seize his weapon from him. The sudden attack sent his foe skidding across the dirt, and he nearly lost his footing. With a sweat-coated brow and veins bulging from his skull, the soldier gnarled his teeth and met the challenge with a raging energy. They jockeyed violently back and forth, neither able to gain the upper hand. As their fingers wrestled for the trigger, a thunderous blast erupted from the barrel and disappeared into the black sky.

In the midst of their hectic dance, Powell raised his revolver and hovered the barrel over his target. A deafening pop shook the trees, and the soldier clutched his side and reeled and swayed. His desperate struggle was in vain, as it was not long until he finally fell upon the rocky terrain and lay still and limp.

It was eerily silent. The men stood frozen and numb, unable to move. Unable to think. They felt nothing, not even the chill air that brushed against their cheeks.

Brennan's voice, soft and trembling, came to their ears. "My God, Henry, what have you done?"

Powell pocketed his revolver and hurried towards the fallen guard. With a heavy sigh, he clamped his burly hands upon the arms and proceeded to drag the corpse towards the embankment.

"What in the hell are you doing?" Collett demanded. "We need to get out of here!"

The planter released his grip and glared at the other three. "I'm the one who's looking out for us." His voice shook. "And if it wasn't for me, y'all would be in their place. Now do me a favor — keep your traps shut and help me get rid of them. Move, damn it!"

They jumped into action quickly and quietly. Before long, the bodies were laid to rest in the creek, directly below the bridge. The men hurried back into their wagons and continued their journey at a much brisker pace. It was a silent ride in the empty darkness, and the only sounds that came to their ears were clicking hooves.

With a trembling hand, Powell lit a cigar and puffed away furiously.

"I didn't mean to sound ungrateful back there," Brennan whispered, his eyes concentrated on the road ahead. "I owe you my life for what you did. I never thought I'd see such a horror unfold before my own eyes…"

"If you're hell-bent on starting a war," the planter said, "then the time will come when *you'll* have to be the one who's willing to pull the trigger."

"I hope I can."

"I hope so too," Powell remarked, "or at the very least, I pray to God you'll have someone by your side who will do it for you."

He let out a long breath and sat back in his chair.

Lord almighty, he brooded in silence. *What's the world coming to?*

Chapter 14

Charleston, South Carolina
November 30, 1860

Emma loathed the attention. Concerned faces studied her as she sat slumped in the carriage, clutching a damp handkerchief. Grace was beside her, offering a comforting hand and gentle reassurances. The tears were beginning to subside, and her thoughts gradually became clearer. What had triggered her emotions was the same lingering feeling that had loomed over her since the summer. For a reason that was eluding her, she missed Streicher a bit more than usual today.

She prayed that it was all a bad dream. That perhaps she would wake up one day, or turn a corner, and he would be waiting for her with a glowing smile and open arms. But the sad reality became more apparent with every new day, and she grew increasingly bitter that she could not change it.

They were parked along a bustling street. Droves of pedestrians past them on both sides, eager to embark on their errands for the day. The early morning sun, bathed in orange, was beginning to emerge above the calm waters of the harbor. Another 'splendid day in this great land of ours,' as Grace liked to say. For Emma, it mattered little whether it rained or shined — all days were unchanging. There was no hope in sight...

She wiped her tear-stained cheeks for the last time and cast a glance towards her cousin. "Forgive me, Grace." She spoke softly. "I don't know what's gotten into me."

"No need to apologize," Grace assured her. "Everyone's entitled to a bad day every now and then."

"These spells seem to be more and more frequent, I'm afraid."

"Be that as it may, cousin, some open air will do you good. I promise."

Their driver, an older Negro man, looked upon her with grave concern. "Y'all be wantin' me te turn 'round 'n' head on home?" he asked.

"No," Emma protested. "I'm fine. Let's enjoy the day."

They joined the crowds and spent the morning popping in and out of dress shops and jewelry stores. Grace tried on a dozen or so outfits — some fashionable and others questionable, which brought an occasional smile to Emma's lips. It was refreshing to feel the light breeze tousle her hair, and Charleston's calm waters allowed her to breathe a bit easier. For the first time in months, she allowed herself to be free from isolation, from being consumed by her pain and dread. Although she did not entirely know how to feel, the experience was certainly better than staying at Uncle Joseph's place.

As the ladies ventured back to their carriage in the waning hours of the afternoon, a peculiar sight caught Emma's attention. A large crowd had gathered in the town square. All eyes were focused upon a small, portly gentleman, who moved about frantically like he had been scorched by a fire. His appearance was almost comical, dressed in a suit and tie that was too tight for his size. Even though he wore a hat, his brow was coated with sweat and his cheeks were stained red.

They made their way over and stood at the rear of the crowd, watching in silence.

"Ladies and gentlemen!" he called out. "Ladies and gentlemen! We have a respectable lot of Negroes for sale today — a respectable lot, indeed! Men, women, children — laborers, drivers, cooks, mechanics. Whatever you're looking for — be it a field hand or a skilled craftsman — I *guarantee* that my slaves will satisfy your needs. Please, step forward and inspect any and all who interest you."

Behind him stood a line of Negroes of varying ages and sizes, all shackled at the wrists and feet. Some looked upon the crowd with wide, fearful eyes; others wept bitterly as if they were sentenced to death. One by one, all interested buyers proceeded slowly down the line, eyeing up prospective hands. The auctioneer raced around from one guest to the next, jumping in at the moment of interest.

"Come on, nigger," he ordered and removed cuffs from a large, burly slave. "Show the gentleman those arms of yours! Cannons, they are! Quite a valuable commodity to have working in your fields, sir, wouldn't you agree?"

Then came a different occasion…

"Abigail, here, will do good work for you," he said, smiling and pulling down the jaw of an older Negro woman, exposing her teeth and gums. "See, sir? She's healthy inside and out. And she makes a splendid apple pie. Wouldn't you like one of her dishes upon your table each night?"

"This lot is quite the package," he remarked in another instance, gesturing to four children and their parents. "They come together — good to keep your family satisfied for two, maybe even three generations. Amos is quite a skilled carpenter — he's built a small church with his own two hands, would you believe it? And Charlotte, what a delight she is, will care for your children like they're her own. If they're anything like their parents, which I ought to reckon they are, the little ones will serve you well for a long time to come. For the right price, sir, they can be yours!"

It was a revolting sight. Yet Emma could not turn her eyes away from it. For as much as her darkest days had loomed over her, it suddenly paled in comparison to the defeated, weary eyes of the slaves. They had experienced horrors that she had never known — that she would never know. And as the auction proceeded, and families were forcefully separated, their pitiful sobs rendered every fiber of her being useless and numb.

"Quite a spectacle, isn't it?" Grace remarked.

"Yes." Emma nodded. "And a despicable one at that."

"They don't know any better, Emma," her cousin said, her voice slightly tense. "They're better off living with a master…"

"Now, here we are, folks!" the auctioneer declared. "Here we are! Boys, why don't you remove those chains and bring Betty on up to the selling block!"

A young Negro woman made her way slowly to a raised platform that overlooked the crowd, head hung low and eyes closed. Like many of the others, her hands and face had been washed, and she cast a bright shine standing under the sun. But she seemed removed from her surroundings, as if she was lost in a dream. She was helped up to the platform, and she faced the onlookers. When her eyes reopened, they showed dark, lifeless beads. Her skin was devoid of its color, and her cheeks were sunken.

"We have ourselves a real prize here," the auctioneer began with a wide smile. "Betty is a recent addition — found her on my way down to this beautiful state, wouldn't you know? She's a quiet one — can slip in and out of a room and you'll hardly know she's there. I reckon she'll do very well as help around the kitchen, or maybe even a hostess if she is properly trained. Now, let's start the bidding at five hundred dollars. Come now, folks! Who would like to acquire this fine Negro? Five hundred dollars! What are my bids?"

Numbers started reeling in one after the other, much to the auctioneer's delight. Five-fifty. Six hundred. Seven-fifty. Higher and higher it went...

Betty stood frozen. Unblinking. Unthinking, or so it seemed. As the bidding surpassed one thousand dollars, Emma began to wonder if she even had a pulse. But then the answer soon became clear...

A gentleman towards the front of the crowd had the winning bid at twelve hundred and fifty dollars. At the sound of 'Sold!' Betty began to sway slowly, her complexion sinking to an even deeper shade of grey.

"My God!" Emma gasped. "She's going to faint..."

It came and went as fast as a bolt of lightning. One moment, the young woman stood before the crowd and then the next, she lay sprawled upon the platform. Several cries erupted from the spectators, and at the sight of trouble, the auctioneer raced over to her. Several patrons also leaped upon the platform, and almost immediately a small group huddled around the fallen slave.

"Wake up, Betty!" the auctioneer cried out. "Come on, girl, don't be giving up on me, you hear!"

Then there were other panicked voices...

"Is she breathing?"

"Someone get a doctor!"

"She's gone cold — she needs medical attention, dammit!"

A doctor eventually arrived upon the scene, but it was too late. Betty lay motionless on the wooden floor, eyes closed. As her body was carried away, the auctioneer stood off to the side and threw his hat upon the ground. He swore bitterly at the loss of what was supposed to be a prosperous sale, but after he let his frustration subside, it was back to the auction block and the bidding resumed to purchase other slaves.

"I don't understand," Emma muttered in disbelief. "That poor girl dropped dead and they're carrying on as if nothing happened."

"Such things happen sometimes." Grace shrugged and commented, "As tragic as it may be, however, it doesn't do the gentleman any good dwelling on his losses."

"Why did she keel over like that?"

"Could have been brought upon by any number of things," was the answer. "Maybe it was her health, or perhaps she was a victim of unfortunate circumstances. In my opinion, for what it's worth, I reckon she came from a cruel owner. There are some Negroes who have that same foggy look about them, like they've been scarred by this business. Every now and then, some of them collapse and that's that. No warning or anything…"

Emma had had enough, and they continued their way back to the carriage. Thought after thought raced into her head, and poor Betty dominated every one of them. There were far too many questions, and a lack of answers left her angry and frustrated.

Who was she? Where did she come from? Did she have a family of her own? What kinds of conditions (dare she even think of it) was she subjected to by her previous owner?

One way or another, it did not make a difference whether she could conceive of any answers. What was done was irreversible, and all she could do was shake her head in disgust.

Heaven help me, she thought bitterly. *What's the world coming to?*

Chapter 15

Brennan Plantation, South Carolina
December 8, 1860

Powell cast his sights upon a fading sun. There was a simple beauty to the night sky, which was lush with purple. A cool breeze scurried through the rolling plains, and his hat twitched slightly. Every now and again, he inhaled a long drag from his cigar, gazing upon the tranquil sights from the back porch. The slaves had retired to their cabins for the night, and he was left to enjoy the beauty of the land.

There was a much different scene inside the mansion. Muffled laughter and jovial banter came to his ears, and every now and again he could make out a word or two. Brennan had decided to host a party, at which every man, woman, and child could 'rejoice in the resiliency and steadfastness of this great state.' There was much for the people of South Carolina to celebrate: by the end of the month, at the very latest, the state legislature would officially declare its secession from the Union. The birth of the Confederacy was imminent.

It was a joyous occasion. An unprecedented affair in only the best of ways. Southern resiliency would prevail, and undoubtedly more states would follow suit. For countless nights, Powell had prayed that Virginia would have the same courage — to make a stand to protect its rights. With the southern gavel ready to strike, there was all too much to take pride in. But for a reason that he struggled to understand, the evening's excitement seemed to pass him by. He could not force a smile. Rather, he needed to step away from it all. The night was better spent in silence…

The back door creaked open, and footsteps approached him. Brennan's voice came to his ears. "Don't tell me that Henry Powell — Richmond's hand-shaking, smooth-talking, socialite extraordinaire — is ready to call it a night!"

"That's your call to make, George, not mine." The planter chuckled, albeit forced. "And for the record, it's Shady Grove — not Richmond."

"Ah, right, Shady Grove." Brennan smiled and put a hand upon his shoulder. "For that, sir, I owe you my sincerest apologies."

"How about you quit your act and that'll suffice instead?"

"Fair enough."

Brennan laughed and lowered his hand. He held a glass of brandy in the other and took a sip. "Taking a break from the action, is that it?" he asked.

"Just taking in the sunset."

"Enjoying yourself?"

"Yes, it's been a fine time."

"You're sure?"

"Of course. Why wouldn't I be?"

"I'm surprised to see you out here by yourself, that's all."

"I'm fine."

"You don't have to lie to me, Henry."

"I'm not…"

"Really." Brennan's smile faded. "I know you — you're usually lost in the crowd, bouncing from person to person. Sharing laughs. Cracking jokes. All that good business… Something troubling you?"

"No."

"Is there *someone* troubling you?"

"No."

"Certain?"

"George." Powell sighed. "Now's not the time for this conversation. You have guests to attend to…"

"Don't worry about them," his friend said, waving a hand. "That's what the help is for. Besides, most of them are two-faced anyway…"

"Is that so?"

"I wish it wasn't." Brennan rolled his eyes. "Anyway, let's get on with it. What's got you down?"

Silence.

"Henry…"

"I know…" Powell raised the cigar to his lips and exhaled. "I had a dream the other night," he began slowly, "rather, a nightmare. It probably doesn't do me any good to dwell on it as much I as I have, but it felt far too real to brush aside…

It was a clear sky and the sun was blazing. I was trapped between large, towering boulders, cradling a rifle in my hands. Cannons thundered and shook the ground so violently that I feared it would crumble beneath me. Speeding bullets threatened me from every angle and chipped away at the rocks. Fresh powder and smoke filled my lungs — I could barely breathe.

I was dressed from head to toe in grey, and my clothes were drenched in sweat. My ears bled from the raging bombardment — I feared I would soon become deaf if this siege lasted any longer. There I was — crouched behind the rocks, clinging to my gun as if it was my child. I looked to my right and saw a young soldier — couldn't have been any more than twenty years old or so — perched above the formation, and he trained his gun upon something and fired away. But as he crouched down to take cover, a bullet tore through his neck and he was thrown back upon the rocks. The earth turned from grey to red instantly.

I fumbled for my rifle — it almost escaped from my hands, they were shaking so terribly. The moment seized me, and it seemed as if I could do nothing more than remain frozen where I was. But then I sprang into action. I struggled for my footing as I scrambled towards lower ground, using the rocks to screen my movement. When I found cover, I peered around the formation and in my midst stood a large hill that led to the sky, or so it seemed. Jagged rocks and boulders were carved in its side, and every now and then men in blue popped up above and around them and rained bullets down upon my position.

My hands steadied themselves, and when the opportunity presented itself, I raised my rifle and returned the favor. Then, immediately, I hid behind the rocks to feed more bullets into the barrel. Fire. Reload. Fire. Reload. On and on it went… and the sun's rays only grew stronger.

I was down to my final bullet, and I feared that if I wasn't struck down by enemy fire sooner or later, the natural elements would certainly do me in. Sweat ran down my brow, and I steadied my hand upon the trigger. I glanced around the boulder and searched frantically to find a speck of blue… but it was too late. Just as my sights elevated to the peak of the hill, towards the sky, I was met by an enemy sniper. His barrel met my eyes, but before I could react, a burst of powder erupted from his position. And just like that — there was only darkness… and then I woke up."

Powell took another draw and held his cigar in a shaking hand. His face was drained of its color.

"Do forgive me." He spoke softly. "I know I shouldn't be spooking myself like this, but it felt far too real for my liking…"

"My friend," Brennan said calmly, "I reckon that run-in we had with those soldiers has gotten into your

237

head. There's nothing to worry about. It was only a dream and nothing more. You're still in one piece, aren't you?"

"I am." The planter laughed nervously. "Maybe you're right — it's been one thing after another lately, hasn't it? I consider myself a resilient man, George, but I must admit it's been a trying time. What I did to those men didn't sit well with me. It still doesn't. But I had no other choice, you understand…"

"Of course," came the reply. "Neither of us would be here today if you hadn't intervened… Look Henry, you're a good friend, and I trust you to keep this between us…"

"Sure."

"I haven't gotten a good night's sleep since Lincoln's victory." Brennan spoke solemnly. "I'm very frightened of the future, if you want the truth…"

"You're not alone," Powell said. "War isn't new to me, George. It's an ugly thing, and there's no way around it… but to have *American* blood on my hands… I don't know — maybe the old ways were too kind to us. We never could have imagined the troubles that would meet us today. For as much as I hate to admit it, I never took the warnings seriously. Bleeding Kansas, Harpers Ferry, they were names and nothing more. Sure, I'll admit I played my part in placing blame upon the North, but it was rhetoric more than anything else. A way to keep my name in the conversation, and Shady Grove ate it up… But I never thought I'd partake in the violence. It was someone else's problem — someone else's battle to fight. But to have the battle come to *me* this time... Well, let's say that it's kept me tossing and turning for some time now."

The two of them stood in silence and gazed upon the horizon.

"I guess I should get back in there, shouldn't I?" Brennan mumbled and gestured towards the door. "Perhaps we shouldn't get too bogged down by our worries. War isn't here yet."

"*Yet*."

"I know."

"See you inside, George."

"Very well, Henry. Take your time..."

He heard the back door creak and then shut. As the sun dipped below the horizon, he finished what was left of his cigar and threw it upon the ground. He stood alone, motionless, with his eyes still fixed upon the night sky. A cool wind whipped his cheeks.

The corners of his lips twitched, and he felt his eyes grow heavy. A string of tears ran down his cheek, and as hard as he tried to fight it, it was no use. The planter fell to his knees and buried his head in his hands. And he wept and wept...

Chapter 16

Charleston, South Carolina
December 20, 1860

Emma cast her sights upon a rising sun. It was a crisp, cool morning, and the steady breeze brushed against her cheeks. She sat perched atop the dock and overlooked the harbor, her legs dangling above choppy waves. Every now and then, a ship came into view, and she followed its course until it was lost in the horizon.

It was in the early morning hours of the day when she felt most at peace, her thoughts clear and collected. Unbeknownst to Uncle Joseph or Grace, she had tiptoed her way out of the house, prepared a carriage, and made her way to the dock. Her actions would undoubtedly be met with strong disapproval from Uncle Joseph, but it mattered little to her. She was a grown woman, and she was certainly capable of making her own decisions. Besides, she needed to be away with her thoughts.

Her pen and diary rested in her lap, and she flipped to a blank page…

December 1860

Thursday, 20th. It is a calm morning, still and silent. Wait a few hours more, and the streets will be jovial and jumping, and fireworks will light up the night sky. Today is a day unlike any other, as if it was the work of a dream. The state legislature will convene to vote upon a declaration of secession, and while I pray that rational minds will prevail, Uncle Joseph says that the Union will dissolve. It is inevitable, he tells me. War is next to come...

I wish I could share the spirit of the optimists. They say that this war, whatever it may bring, will be brief and forever put to rest this country's divisions. But I do not share the sentiment. Blood has already been shed, and more lives are doomed to perish. Neither side is to be a victor. All will bear the consequences.

It doesn't help much to dwell on the happenings of the outside world. My own is trouble enough...

Often, I have dreams of looking out upon sunny skies and lush grasses, tucked away from the rest of the world. Erich and I live in an old log cabin, where we raise our two children — one boy and one girl — and we haven't a care in the world. Then I wake up...

I never thought much of fate. For as long as I could remember, life carried me away like the current of the sea. Without a particular course or destination. But now, as my own world — and all its hopes and possibilities — lies shattered, I cannot help but question the meaning of my suffering. Perhaps it would be best to escape from it all, as it is too apparent that my best days are far behind me. Even now, as I'm writing, I feel tempted to take the leap and let myself be consumed by the depths below. Only then will my dream, a taste of Heaven perhaps, come true.

Emma paused. Tears flowed steadily down her cheeks, and her pen shook in her hand. She longed to put more words to the paper, to put an encouraging spin on her tragic tale and right too many wrongs. But she was at a loss…

The past was unchangeable, and the future, unfathomable. It was a trap, and she hated that there were no brighter days ahead. Her eyes scanned the dark depths that beckoned to her, and she placed her notebook aside and very slowly, steadily, raised herself to her feet. The tips of her shoes dangled above the raging waters…

Her breaths grew heavier, and as she closed her eyes, she embraced every feeling in her body: the gentle sway of her hair as it whipped against the breeze, her racing heart, and the fire in her lungs.

Only a step away, she told herself. *Only one step…*

Time stood still.

Her feet remained where they stood.

"Emma." A gentle voice came to her ears. "Don't start thinking that you can get away from me that easily…"

Her eyes opened, and suddenly she felt a warm hand coil around her wrist. She turned and gazed into twinkling, calm blue eyes.

Streicher stood draped in rags, his hair tousled and mangy, and his face coated with dirt. A friendly smile came across his lips, and tears traveled down his cheeks. "How about you step down from there, alright?"

Without thought, she threw herself at him and the two of them wrapped each other in their arms. She rested her head upon his shoulder and embraced a moment that she could have only dreamed of... but it was real! His touch was warm and reassuring, and his heart pounded as quickly as hers. Through heavy sobs, she gazed upon him with glistening eyes and a radiant smile. She longed to find the right words to say, but all she could do was look upon him with wondrous delight.

"Pardon my appearance." Streicher chuckled as the tears flowed down his cheeks. "I haven't exactly been living the fine life these last few months."

"H-How?" mouthed Emma.

"I was told you'd been living down here with your uncle," he said, "and I couldn't wait for you to return to the city." He chuckled and added, "I couldn't even stop to get a fresh change of clothes."

How? she repeated to herself, too overcome with disbelief to process his words. But he was here and that was all that mattered.

"Abolitionists vouched for me," he continued. "Scores of them came out of the woodwork and

243

declared my innocence — day in and day out they petitioned the court to acquit me of any sort of involvement in your father's death. They denounced the 'evidence' brought against me as corrupt, which it was in every sense of the word. But the judge wouldn't give in. Well, someone — a congressman, I believe — must've eventually played the right strings because a five-thousand-dollar check made its way to his desk, or so the rumor goes. In any case, what was done was enough. My sentence was changed to a misdemeanor charge: public drunkenness and petty theft (don't ask me where he came up with that one). I guess the judge wanted to save face a bit, but I'm grateful that my 'friends' carried a bit more weight than your father's. In exchange for a trip to the gallows, I got three months behind bars. And I would've gotten off sooner if the case wasn't so political. Nonetheless, the charges were dropped as soon as my time was served… and now, by the grace of God, I am a free man!"

Her heart raced faster than ever before. It was all so sudden, too surreal to grasp. Yet he stood before her with that same warm smile, calm and inviting, and he held her in his arms. She did not want him to let go, not for anything in the entire world. How he came to escape his fate, which seemed so inevitable, she could not fathom. More than anyone, she knew her father's 'associates' were men who flaunted power and influence… and they had wanted revenge. Even she, admittedly, wanted Doyle brought to justice, even if it meant he would hang. But Streicher... he was innocent. There was never any doubt in her mind; there never would be any doubt.

"Emma." Streicher's smile faded. "I never wanted this for us. Believe me, it was *never* my intention to hurt your father. If I had known what Doyle was going to do, I would've stopped him *long* before we ever came to your door. Everything slipped out of hand so quickly... I had no time to react. I'm so..."

"Don't be." Her voice quivered. "Please, Erich, you are the *last* person who should apologize for anything..."

"I feel like I should..."

"Doyle, certainly," Emma said through tear-filled eyes, "but not you."

"Well, if it's Doyle you're concerned about," he responded, his face slightly ashen, "don't be. He wasn't as lucky as I was. Apparently, he spent his final moments swearing up and down that slavery was to be the death of us all."

He shook his head and struggled to fight back tears. "Christ," he said, fuming. "It probably will be. This country's on the brink of war, isn't it?"

"I don't care about that." Emma met his gaze. "Not about slavery, states' rights, none of it. Not anymore."

"I want to start fresh," Streicher said. "That's all. Move to the countryside somewhere, just like we always wanted to. Live a quiet life. Humble. Where it's only you and me..."

She was saved. In the blink of an eye, it seemed, life had regained its purpose. There was a future to look out for, to be excited about. Time would heal old wounds; she just needed to be patient. There was a reason to smile again, and for that alone she would be forever grateful. "Who's to say that can't happen?"

"You'll come with me then?"

"Of course." Emma nodded excitedly. "Tell me where and I'll follow you…"

"I love you." He spoke softly and squeezed her in his arms. "I've missed you so much…"

Emma rested her head upon his shoulder and savored the comfort of his embrace. The world around her was suddenly irrelevant, not worthy of her attention. All that mattered was that they were together, and that their future was anything but broken. She cast a cheerful glance to the sky, as if to acknowledge some unseeing presence. A silent protector.

Thank you. Thank you, thank you, thank you…

And she wept and wept…

Epilogue

Powell Plantation, Virginia
April 3, 1865

The parlor was dark and silent. Cold air chilled the halls, and the misery of the day brought along a sense of dread and discomfort. Powell sat slumped in an armchair before a crackling fire, which cast the only light in the entire mansion. Gentle heat warmed his cheeks, but he felt none of it. Heavy rain pattered above the ceiling, and soft rumbling echoed in the distance. Every now and then, his glassy eyes swayed to a small table beside him, and he reached for a glass of brandy, his movements rigid and forced.

He was consumed by his thoughts. His terrors. The war had raged on far longer than he could ever have imagined, and on many nights he drank himself to sleep. Liquid courage was the best medicine. The *only* medicine, it seemed, that enabled him to live in a world that knew only suffering and hardship.

Maybe he should have been grateful. After all, his property had been spared a visit by Yankee artillery. Many of Shady Grove's residents, however, were not so lucky. At the outbreak of the war, Union soldiers had stormed through the small town, and though they were met with some resistance, it was not enough to repel the onslaught. Dozens of men, young and old, had perished in the conflict, and the town was quickly plundered and set ablaze. Powell knew he should have fought alongside them, leading the charge, but instead he locked himself away in the walls of his mansion and let it pass him by, much as he would a raging storm. Such was his conduct throughout the whole course of the war, and he slept well at night knowing that others were fighting the battles for him.

Violence was no longer the means to achieve any sort of resolution, he was convinced, but his stance was not met well by his neighbors. The entire town had turned against him, and they had branded him a 'spineless coward'. What did it matter to him, anyway? His true friends, those who had real meaning in his life, knew nothing about Shady Grove's troubles.

Powell sighed as he stared down into his glass. There was an absence of laughter in the room. He wished he could rekindle the past, turn the clocks back with a snap of his fingers to a much simpler time. A much more pleasant time. But he could not be fooled. More than anyone, he knew there was no turning back. What was gone was gone forever, and he had lost enough…

Herman Knouse, his wartime companion during the days of the Mexican War, thought it best to escape from the conflict altogether and return overseas to Germany. He did not blame him for doing so; that was the smarter choice.

Edward Collett had joined the ranks of the South Carolina infantry shortly after the siege of Fort Sumter. For over a year, the two of them had exchanged correspondence. Initially, Collett had expressed his frustrations as a soldier, describing it in one instance as a 'monotonous plight, miserable and deprived of any comforts.' It was not until September of 1862 that his words offered promise. There was action anticipated near Sharpsburg, Maryland, and he vowed to 'give the Yanks a hell of a fight.' That was the last he had heard from his dear friend, and the details surrounding his final moments were left to his imagination. It was better off that way.

Then there was George Brennan, his closest friend. A brother. Like Collett, he found a place among South Carolina's ranks. Brennan had paraded around with a sense of duty and commitment, remarking in one letter that his decision to join the Confederate Army was 'one of the proudest moments of my life.' He gave hope to his company and led them forward with a triumphant spirit, even on days that were long and bitter. Or so the story went...

In the summer of 1863, Powell no longer received his letters. As fate would have it, the planter later learned from other sources, Brennan fell at the Battle of Gettysburg. Allegedly, he had been pinned down behind rocky terrain and was faced with an unrelenting volley of enemy fire. As he crept out to return a volley of his own, he was struck down by a marksman's bullet.

Of all the tragedies that the war brought with it, Brennan's death was the worst of them. It was a loss that sent the planter spiraling into a deep depression, and he eventually became dependent upon the bottle.

There was a time when life was something to celebrate, to enjoy with friends. But after a while, somehow, almost everything he cherished near and dear to him was snatched away. He was forced to free his slaves as Union forces began to take control of the state. There were several who remained at his plantation, earning feeble wages as they tended to the fields. But many, including his most highly regarded workers like Rose and Sampson, had set off to find new lives in the North.

Even his dear wife, his last hope for pleasure and joy, was bedridden with a terrible fever. It was only a matter of time before she would take her last breaths…

Might as well call it quits now, he thought as he took a swill from his glass. *Looks like the sun's fading on you real quick, Henry.*

A loud knock freed him from his miserable stupor, and he begrudgingly made his way to the front door. When he swung it open, a young man met him with a friendly smile. His blonde hair was neatly combed and his clothes, finely pressed. A satchel was slung across his shoulder, and he held an envelope in his hand.

"Good afternoon, sir," he said. "You are Mr. Powell, I presume?"

"You've presumed correctly," Powell remarked flatly and eyed his hand. "Got something for me, eh?"

"I do." He extended the envelope. "A letter from Maryland, I believe."

"Thanks."

"Certainly."

"So, you're the new mail carrier, is that it?"

"I am, sir."

"What's your name, son?"

"Streicher," he responded and held out his hand. "Erich Streicher."

They shook. "It's a pleasure, Streicher."

"Likewise, sir."

"You're new to the area, I take it?"

"That's right," Streicher nodded. "I lived in South Carolina for a few years, outside of Charleston. But I'm originally from Philadelphia."

"A Yankee living in the South?" the planter sneered. "You're brave, son. Very brave."

"Rest assured, sir, I don't intend to start another war," Streicher said, laughing. "In fact, I'd like to stay as far away from all of it as much as possible. Too much bad business, if you ask me."

"Yes." Powell took another sip. "I reckon you've got some wits about you."

"Not all the time, I'm afraid."

"I wish I could say I was any different," was the response, "but if I did, I'd be lying to you."

The two of them chuckled.

"Anyhow, Streicher," the planter began, "where are you living now?"

"Right here in Shady Grove with my wife and children."

"Ah, very nice — how old are the rascals?"

"I've got a son — he's three years old," Streicher answered, "and my daughter celebrated her first birthday in January."

"Wonderful." Powell smiled gently and raised his glass. "Here's to you…"

"Thank you, sir."

"Whereabouts in Shady Grove are you living?"

"On the outskirts," he stated. "We live in an old cabin. Can't say much for the size of it, but it comes with a nice piece of land — even has a large barn too. From what I understand, it belonged to a farmer and his wife."

"The McLearys." Powell spoke slowly. "Yes, they had been there for quite some time…"

"What a shame about Mr. McLeary, isn't it?"

Silence.

"I take it you've heard about…"

"I have."

Silence.

"Well, Mr Powell." Streicher spoke uneasily. "I'd best be on my way. Have a good rest of the day."

"You do the same."

Powell closed the door behind him and became submerged in darkness. Thomas McLeary. The name only conjured harsh memories and a piece of his past that he wished he could bury forever. But for as much as he tried to suppress it, to clear it from his mind, sooner or later it came flooding back to him. He should have never resorted to such violent methods, but there was no sense in drowning himself in remorse. Like everything else, what was done was done. There was nothing he could do to make amends...

And then there was Alice. She had moved back to Richmond, or so he had heard. Maybe there was still a chance, be it ever so small, that he could have a future with her. All that was needed was for his wife to...

You're a selfish son of a bitch, aren't you? He scolded himself. *Enough of that...*

He made his way back into the parlor and propped himself into his chair. The glow of the fire illuminated his pale, sunken features, and he raised the envelope and tore it open. His eyes strained as he began to read:

Dear Henry,

I trust that you are a man of action, and it is for that reason that I am writing to you with an urgent request. As you are aware, our country is on the verge of collapse, threatened by encroaching Union guns. More than ever, an immediate and decisive response is needed to restore the spirit of our cause. Such a feat, I fear, is no longer feasible upon a battlefield. The war must come directly to those who are responsible for it, and they must be silenced.

Under my direction, there is a group of able-bodied recruits who are willing to do what is necessary to sustain the war effort. Although our numbers are small, a man of your stature would be a valuable asset to us. Keep all correspondence between us confidential, and if such a worthy pursuit would be of interest to you, you know where to send the letter.

Death to tyrants!
J. Wilkes Booth

Powell polished off his brandy. Calmly, carefully, he folded the letter and tucked it into the envelope.

I never would've guessed you had a flair for dramatics, John, he chuckled as he tossed the envelope into the fire. *That'll be the day...*

It was time for another drink.